EBURY PRESS

AGHORI

A motivational speaker, leadership coach and behavioural trainer by profession, Mayur Kalbag's hobby of writing poetry and prose evolved into a serious avocation twelve years ago, after he returned from a trip to Kailash Mansarovar along with his guru, Swami Sadyojat Shankarashram.

Mayur has written two books of poetry: *Smile at Stress* and *Rising Waterfall*. His first book of prose, *Adventures of Poorna*, was well received by readers.

Mayur is also a passionate artist and has made his mark in the abstract and contemporary genre with art exhibitions in India and Switzerland.

An adventurer at heart, Mayur is an avid trekker and rock climber.

Apart from all this, his true passion is imagining, visualizing, exploring and then articulating new realms of philosophical fiction and spiritualism through the process of writing.

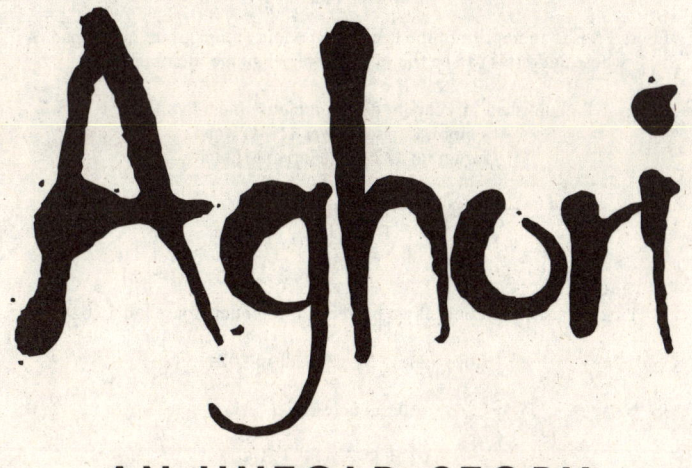

Aghori

AN UNTOLD STORY

MAYUR KALBAG

EBURY
PRESS

An imprint of Penguin Random House

EBURY PRESS

Ebury Press is an imprint of the Penguin Random House group of companies
whose addresses can be found at global.penguinrandomhouse.com

Published by Penguin Random House India Pvt. Ltd
4th Floor, Capital Tower 1, MG Road,
Gurugram 122 002, Haryana, India

Penguin
Random House
India

First published in Ebury Press by Penguin Random House India 2024

ISBN 9780143468462

Typeset in Sabon LT Std by Manipal Technologies Limited, Manipal
Printed at Thomson Press India Ltd, New Delhi

www.penguin.co.in

MIX
Paper | Supporting
responsible forestry
FSC® C010615

The love and guidance of my guru, Swami Sadyojat Shankarashram, along with the teachings He has imparted to me, have been the true inspiration for all my passionate pursuits—one of them being writing poetry and prose. Swamiji's love and blessings have been the wind beneath my wings that let me fly to different and unexplored horizons of thoughts and imagination, and truly has enabled me to write my stories and compose my poems. His words of wisdom have been the oxygen to keep my mind vibrantly awakened, and for it to think not just outside the box but above it!

I dedicate my book, Aghori: An Untold Story, *to my beloved guru, who means more than the world to me, and whom I love and respect from the depths of my heart.*

Preface

Aghori: An Untold Story is a vibrantly coloured collage of the varied experiences that the protagonist, Subraiya, or Subbu as he is fondly called, goes through. Subbu's deep and earnest desire to know more about the Aghori sadhus/babas becomes the basis of this most unique and indelible journey of adventures and experiences.

The book is not just a story but also an opportunity for the reader to experience an exuberant expedition that incorporates diverse activities which are spiritual, intriguing, ethereal and, at times, frightening!

Aghori: An Untold Story has been written in the first person because I wanted to make the reader feel that they are an intrinsic part of all the adventures and experiences. I believe that it is completely up to the reader—or a better word would be the 'viewer'—to infer whether the story of Subbu and his journey with the Aghoris is fiction or reality!

1

Gouge the Eye Out!

'Take that knife, not the small one, the bigger one, yeah, the one that is near the fire. Okay good, now what you have to do is to gently gouge the left eye out of the socket and remember, you have to do this in one action.' It was the Aghori baba, and as he gave me instructions, I was sweating as well as shivering with nervousness. The corpse was half burnt and I was sitting right in front of it, about to gouge its left eye out.

'You seem reluctant,' the baba exclaimed. He suddenly came towards me, snatched the knife from me and brought it close to my neck, almost as if he wanted to stab me. His face was just a couple of inches away from mine and he was looking straight at me, or rather, into my eyes.

He closed his eyes for a few seconds and began muttering something, and then he opened his eyes

1

again. I was completely stunned to see that the colour of his eyeballs and the retina had turned jet black. He still had the knife to my throat!

'My boy, I know that you have a very strong heart and I appreciate your keenness to know more about the Aghori *siddhi* (knowledge of the Aghori science). And so, if you wish for that to happen, you should stay with me for seven days and learn a few significant aspects of this *vidya* (knowledge). If you don't wish to stay with me, then leave right now! Tell me, what is your decision?'

Without hesitating even a wee bit, I nodded and whispered to him, 'I shall stay with you.'

Hearing this, he took the knife away from my throat and in a swift move, gouged out the left eye of the corpse, stood up and started shouting, '*Aulaakh Niranjan*', a few times.

As he walked away, he said, 'Next time, if and when I tell you to do something, you will not say no to me. Now, come with me, let me show you your chamber as that is where you will be staying the rest of the week.'

'What about this?' I asked, pointing at the partially burnt dead body.

'I will have it later,' he said with a smirk.

I stood up and followed him as he walked out of the cremation ground towards what looked like a dilapidated temple. It almost looked haunted.

'What are you worried about? Just come and have some *ras* (juice) with me. We will eat later,' he said, in a seemingly affectionate tone. I was quite sure that he had felt the fear and nervousness in my every action.

* * *

It was my first day at the Kotisurya village, the one which was known for the many Aghori sadhus who lived there. This village was close to Haridwar in the north of India. I had reached it from Haridwar by bullock cart as none of the cabs were interested in taking me there. Some said that the entire village was haunted and a few demanded a lot of money to take me there. There was one particular taxi driver who asked me why I was so keen to go to the village that was infamous for being haunted.

'Sir, I am extremely keen to learn about the life of the Aghori sadhus and I got to know from the Internet that the village of Kotisurya was the best place to find them,' I told him.

'But you must be totally out of your mind. No one goes there. It is haunted for sure. I myself have seen ghosts. I think it is better you go to some other place to see the Aghori sadhus. In fact, there are a few cremation grounds here in Haridwar itself where you could get a glimpse of the Aghori babas, and I am sure they will let you ask whatever questions you wish to ask them.'

As the taxi driver was saying all this to me, I could not help notice a teenager standing by the roadside, staring at me; he seemed to be smiling at me. The taxi driver was now busy telling me about the other wonderful places near Haridwar, but my mind was distracted by the teenager who was continuously staring at me. He was making me slightly uncomfortable.

Finally, I politely stopped the taxi driver and walked directly towards the teenager. As I got near him, he greeted me with folded hands and offered to take me to the village.

'Sahib, pardon me, but I was eavesdropping on your conversation with the taxi driver. I can see that you are very sincere about your intent to go to the village to see and meet the Aghori sadhus. I am a farmer from Kotisurya village and I come to the main vegetable market of Haridwar to sell my weekly produce. I am returning to the village in another hour and if you are interested, I can take you there with me. Having said this, the only issue is that I don't have a taxi, but you will surely love the ride on my bullock cart. Sahib, I will charge you two hundred rupees for it. Are you interested?' he asked with an intense expression.

My initial reaction was to doubt him. I was also a bit taken aback by the fact that he was the only one who was willing to take me there.

How can he so openly offer me the ride? Is there something fishy? I thought.

The boy tapped me on my shoulder and said, 'Sahib, the village is not haunted at all. These taxi drivers and a lot of people from this town fear the Aghori sadhus, and for good reason. Twenty years ago, three people from here went to the village and never returned. When two policemen came to our village to probe the matter, they returned with their skeletons. The rumour is that they were eaten alive by the Aghori sadhus because they had angered them by throwing stones at them while they were performing an important tantric ritual. Since then, not a single person from this town goes to the village as they fear the Aghoris. I hail from the same village, and I can tell you for a fact that the Aghori sadhus live in a certain part of the village. They are actually very peaceful people and mind their own business. In fact, they come and help us out whenever required. But then, they are extremely angry people as well, and if they are disturbed or troubled, then they can go to any extent to express their anger. And as regards the three men being eaten alive, that was not what happened. The truth is that they were eaten by wild animals and not by the Aghoris. I can see that you have a lot of genuine interest in knowing about them and hence I felt I must offer you a ride to the village. I am asking for two hundred rupees because we are poor and don't have enough hard cash with us. A bit of additional money will help,' the teenager said.

Somehow, although I had met this person only a few moments ago, I began to believe he was honest. 'Okay, I will take up your offer. But then, how will I come back?' I asked.

'That is something you don't have to worry about. Tomorrow morning, I will bring you back as I have to return to the market to buy some essential things for my farm,' he said.

'Tomorrow? Then what about my stay? I have booked a room in a hotel here and my luggage is also here,' I said in an anxious tone.

'Why do you worry, sahib? You please stay with me in my house. We have enough rooms to accommodate you. In fact, you will get to know a lot more about the Aghoris or Aghori babas from my father. And I will not charge you a single penny for your stay with us. Regarding your luggage, we still have an hour—you can go and get whatever you need for the overnight stay,' he said with a big smile.

I was in two minds. On the one hand, I was extremely keen to go and see the Aghoris, and on the other, I was unsure as I would have to stay overnight in some village and at the house of someone whom I had just met. 'Okay, thank you. I will stay with you tonight,' I said to him finally. I was keen and did not want to miss the opportunity to learn about the Aghoris from his father. I quickly went to the hotel, packed a few clothes and some essentials in my haversack and told the hotel manager that I would be back the next day.

He seemed a bit perplexed and asked me where I was heading.

'I have got a lift to Kotisurya village to meet the Aghoris,' I told him.

'Sir, why are you doing this? That place is haunted and people who have gone there have not returned.

But, if you are going, then please do me one big favour. If you do meet any Aghori sadhu, please ask him for his blessing for me and my wife. We have been married for more than ten years and have not had a child despite undergoing medical treatment. I have been told that their blessings have tremendous power,' he said.

I was quite surprised at his request. 'Hey, tell me something. In the many years you have been living here, you know that many people from Kotisurya come to Haridwar, and yet are you asking me to get the blessings from the Aghoris! You could have asked the villagers a long time ago, right? I am sure they would have got it for you,' I exclaimed.

'Sir, you think I have not tried? Of course, I have! But then, the villagers don't heed my request. They keep giving silly reasons. Hence, I thought I could ask you since you are going to the village especially to meet the Aghoris.'

The manager seemed rather desperate. He was almost pleading with me and I felt bad for him. I assured him that I would try my best. I told him that I myself was unaware of what to expect. Before I left, he touched my feet.

'What are you doing, sir? Why are you touching my feet?' I reacted spontaneously. I was taken aback and a bit angry at his gesture. He was much older than me and I did not like him touching my feet.

'Sir, I am touching your feet because you are doing something no one has done before. Even some photographers from foreign countries refused to go into the village after being told about the hauntings. Some adventurous explorers who still wanted to go could not as there was no one to take them. One of them tried to trek through the forested road but was attacked by what he says were demonic beings. He somehow managed to return, but he had deep scratch marks on his back and neck. I truly applaud you for the sincere courage you are showing to go to that village and meet the Aghoris,' he said.

'Is there something I need to be scared about?' I asked him. His compliments to me about my courage were beginning to make me feel a bit fearful now. But I had to go—meeting and interacting with the Aghori babas was something I had been dreaming about since my schooldays.

'No sir, to be honest, I am sure that adventurer was attacked by sloth bears, which are in plenty in the forests outside the village. He could not have seen any demonic beings as it was *Amavasya* (no moon night).'

By the time my conversation was over, I heard the teenager calling out for me. 'Sahib! We need to go. If we wait any longer, we will reach the village late in the night. There are lots of bears and we don't want any encounters with them on our way.'

The boy's words actually made me feel a bit relieved. *So, no demonic beings for sure*, I thought to myself. I assured the hotel manager about seeking blessings for him and his wife, walked out and hopped on to the bullock cart. I was finally on my way to Kotisurya, to meet the Aghoris.

2

Rahasya Is My Name, and That Is a Secret!

'Sahib, please come here, next to me. That way you will see the route much better and we can talk through the journey as well.'

I happily scrambled my way to the front. Although there wasn't much space for both of us to sit, I did not mind because I had a lot of questions to ask him and was also getting a better view of the countryside.

As we proceeded towards the village, we began conversing.

'Sahib, tell me something. How did you come to know about the village and especially about the Aghoris from Kotisurya?' he asked me with an intense note in his tone. 'Not many people know about them or about my village,' he added.

I had sort of known this question was going to come my way. 'First, can I know your name?' I asked.

'Yes, sahib. My name is Rahasya. It means a secret,' he replied.

I thought, *what kind of a name is that?*

'Sahib, this name was given to me by one of the senior-most Aghori sadhus. I therefore have to keep it. What I am telling you is a rahasya or secret, so please don't tell anyone.' Saying this, he started laughing heartily.

I looked at him a bit perplexed, and decided to answer his question about how I had heard about his village. 'Rahasya, a few years ago, while I was working for a sweater manufacturing company, I got a chance to go to Rishikesh. I had been sent by my company to meet a few customers who had shown interest in buying our products.'

'What products, sahib?' he interrupted with his pleasant curiosity.

'Well, our company was into the manufacturing and sales of woollen sweaters and some shops in Rishikesh were our wholesale dealers. So, my colleagues and I were at Rishikesh on work. One evening, after my meeting with the customers, while I was returning to my hotel by taxi, I saw something strange. Two men who looked like sadhus were seated on the side of the road shouting *"Har Har Mahadeva Shambho"*. As we drove past, one of them looked straight at me and he actually called me by my name. For a second, I was totally stunned. I told the taxi driver to stop the car, which he was reluctant to do. I wanted to know who this person was and how he knew my name. The taxi driver told me that it was not safe to stop in the middle of nowhere. I requested him to stop just for a while.

'"One of them shouted my name and I don't even know him," I said to the driver.

'"Sahib, these are Aghori babas and they are very powerful. I am not surprised that they know your name just by seeing you for a second. Sir ji, please let us go. I am getting scared. These Aghoris are capable of anything. Please let us leave right now."

'I realized the taxi driver was extremely nervous and said okay. It was just then I heard one of the babas shouting again. "We will meet, but after a year and in my cave. Now, you go to your hotel and sleep well or else I will come and beat you up. And don't forget to offer my *pranams* to your Guru Shankara when you see him next month for the Holi festival."

'I was looking at the Aghori baba who was shouting all this to me, and then, to my utter shock, both of them stood up and started charging towards our vehicle. Before I could say anything to the driver, he accelerated and we were off.

'*How did he know about my guru, and to add to that, he also knew about my upcoming visit to my native place, Bailooran!* I thought to myself.

'The taxi driver seemed quite shaken up by the two babas charging towards us, but we soon left them behind. As I got down from the taxi, he looked at me and told me to return home as soon as possible. I asked him why.

'"Sir ji, it looks like they have spotted you or they probably have some business with you."

'"Business?" I asked.

'"Business means I think they have something they want to give you or take from you," he clarified.

'All this was confusing and a bit terrifying for me. Back in my room, I ensured that the door and the windows were properly locked. Even while having dinner at a restaurant near the hotel, I couldn't stop myself from looking around once in a while, hoping not to see them. That entire night, I constantly thought about my unexpected encounter with the Aghori sadhus.

'The next day, I had to go to another customer but via the same route and with the same taxi driver. Interestingly, he sent someone else saying that he had fever. I realized he must have been quite scared, although I felt he had really no reason to feel nervous and fearful as it was me who the Aghori baba was shouting at.

'That night too I couldn't sleep well as the encounter with the baba kept haunting my mind. However, I felt this earnest desire to meet them. In the wee hours of the morning, I finally fell into deep sleep and that is when I had a dream and, guess what?'

'What, sahib?' Rahasya asked anxiously.

'In that dream, I saw the same Aghori babas I had encountered on the roadside in the middle of nowhere. They were in my room and were speaking to me. Surprisingly, I seemed to be quite calm and in fact, happy to be with them. "*Balak* (child), don't feel nervous about being with us. We may look scary to you, but we are like coconuts, hard on the outside but extremely soft on the inside. Last night, we were just having some fun with you by scaring you. Now, listen to me very carefully. After you come to our village, Kotisurya, you will initially face a few difficulties to reach us, but it is important that you meet us as this has to do with your guru. Please understand, it is your guru who needs something that is available only with us. It has to do with a specific meditation practice. You will know the details only when you meet us next year. We have come here to let you know that there is no reason to fear us. So tomorrow, when you are returning from your customer's office, you will not see us because our mission has been accomplished. We will meet at Kotisurya next year. We bless you, balak. *Aulaakh Niranjan, Aulaakh Niranjan!*"

'Saying this, they came close to me, touched my forehead and then pinched me hard on my right arm, so hard that I woke with a shudder. It was almost 7 a.m. and sunlight had already filled the room. I was sure that it had not been a dream, but had really happened, because I was literally experiencing a sharp pain in my right arm. *Did it happen? Did they actually pinch me?* I wondered. I jumped out of bed and rushed to the washbasin to look in the mirror there. I removed my T-shirt and, guess what? There was a red mark on my right arm and, to my further shock, I noticed it was not just an ordinary pinch mark. It looked exactly like a small version of the spiritual symbol known as *Aum*.'

'What are you saying, sahib? This is unbelievable!' Rahasya reacted with shock and fear. I immediately pulled the right sleeve of my T-shirt up and then what he saw made him pull on the reins and stop the bullock cart. The Aum symbol was still there from the time I was pinched in my dream by the Aghoris. Rahasya stopped the bullock cart and kept looking at me.

'Sahib, you have been blessed by them and nothing will ever be able to attack or hurt you. I have heard about the Aghoris pinching some people and then the pinch mark would take the shape of a very significant spiritual symbol, just like the one you have on your right arm! Let me tell you one thing, sahib. Although I have heard stories about this from my father and also from my grandfather, this is the first time I am actually seeing it.' Saying this, the boy quite spontaneously touched my feet and asked me to bless him.

'Rahasya, I am just a normal person, so how can I bless you, my friend?' I told him with a smile.

'Sahib, you are very special. Not many in this world have been blessed by the Aghoris, especially in the way you have been. Please bless me with happiness and lots of money,' he said.

I did not know what to do. I had never blessed anyone before. I was only twenty-nine—not old enough or wise enough to bless someone, I thought to myself. Rahasya seemed extremely keen though, and so I simply prayed to my guru to bless him with all that he desired.

'Sahib, please touch my head,' he pleaded. With slight reluctance, I did as he asked.

'Can we please go to the village now, Rahasya?'

'Yes, sahib. For sure,' he replied smiling, and we were back in motion.

3

The Sloth Bears

The road to the village and the areas surrounding it were extremely rustic. The time was approximately 5 p.m., and we were half an hour into the journey. We were travelling through a dense forested area, and due to the lack of sunlight, it was dark everywhere.

'How long before we reach your village?' I asked Rahasya.

'Sahib, we should be entering the village within the next hour. By taxi, it takes just about forty-five minutes,' he answered. He added, 'Sahib, what I plan to do is drop you at the place from where you will be able to meet the Aghori sadhus sooner rather than later.'

'And where is this place you plan to drop me?' I asked with slight hesitation.

'Sahib, that will be at the cremation ground, which is just a few kilometres outside our village. Once you are done with the meeting, call me from your cell phone and I will come to pick you up and take you to my house. Will that be okay?'

'That sounds great,' I replied with a wry smile. The last place I would want to be was at a cremation ground, but I was aware of one important fact, which was that the Aghoris spend most of their time at cremation grounds. Therefore, if I had to meet them, then I had to be brave!

Sitting on a bullock cart was a very different experience, and I was thoroughly enjoying it. All of a sudden, Rahasya stopped the cart. 'Can you hear it?' he asked in a whisper.

'What?' I replied, quite curious.

'Sahib, listen carefully!' he said softly. I nodded. Initially, all I could hear were the sounds of leaves rustling in the wind and then, I heard something different. It definitely sounded like a grunt. 'Did you hear it?' he asked.

'Oh, yes, I did!' I told him excitedly.

'Look, sahib, there are four of them! Can you see them?' he said, pointing towards our left. I looked intently and what I saw was simply astonishing!

There they were, four sloth bears only ten feet away from us. Two of them looked like cubs and I assumed the other two were their parents. To my surprise, they stepped out on the road and came close to us. Immediately, Rahasya reached into his pocket and pulled out something that looked like sugar-coated candy, and then to my utter shock, he began feeding them. I could not believe what I was witnessing. Four wild bears were eating candy given by this young boy.

'Sahib, why don't you feed them as well?' Saying this, he almost forcibly placed a few candies in my hand. 'Don't get scared, sahib, they are quite docile with humans because we regularly use this route. That large male standing closest to you? I have seen him since he was a baby bear. We almost grew up together. Sahib, don't worry at all. Just place a few candies on your palm, stretch it towards them and the bears will take them without you even feeling it.' Rahasya tried his best to convince me, but I was absolutely unwilling to do what he said.

'Hey, Rahasya, I am definitely not feeding these wild bears. Come, we need to reach soon and I suggest we resume our journey.' I was not only apprehensive but quite scared. I had never come so close to bears, and that too wild ones. The last time I had seen sloth bears was in a zoo.

Rahasya realized the urgency and also my state of nervousness and so we resumed our journey. Finally, he brought the bullock cart to a halt. 'Sahib, just about half a kilometre from here is the cremation ground. Unfortunately, I cannot take you any further as there is really no pathway for my cart,' he told me in a slightly apologetic tone. 'Don't worry, sahib. Just follow the path you see right there and you will come to a small temple. It is the Aghori temple and it is also the entry point to the cremation ground. I hope you get to meet them and find whatever you have come here for,' he added.

I alighted from the bullock cart, put my haversack on my back and, after bidding goodbye to Rahasya, I started hiking towards the cremation ground. As I walked on the narrow path, I could not help but smile about a very strange thing. I thought to myself, just a while ago I was so nervous and scared to feed the wild sloth bears, and here I am, walking to a cremation ground to meet the Aghoris, completely fearless; rather, with a heightened sense of excitement!

4

Flames from My Palm

Although I was quite literally walking through a dense forest, presumably with wild animals around, including the sloth bears, it seemed unusually calming and peaceful. The only thought in my head was to meet the Aghori sadhus and get the thing that my guru had asked me for, and this kept me from feeling any kind of fear. After walking for about fifteen minutes, I came across a temple. *This must be the same Aghori temple that Rahasya was telling me about*, I thought. It seemed to be a very ancient structure but it was surely a temple.

I decided to go inside and pray to the deity and then venture further into the cremation ground to meet the Aghoris. I took off my shoes, walked up the steps and entered a room where I saw what looked like an idol of a god. Two oil lamps were placed in two corners of the room. Despite it still being daylight outside, the room was almost dark; the only light came from the two steadily burning flames of the oil lamps. Taking a closer look, I realized that the idol was of a yogi or a Himalayan monk in a standing position. Although my initial intention was to prostrate myself before the idol, seek blessings and proceed further, for some unexplainable reason I decided to sit in that room for some more time. So, I kept my bag in a corner and sat right in front of the deity. I pulled out my *japamala* (prayer beads), took a few deep breaths and started chanting the mantra, initially aloud and then silently.

This was definitely not part of my plan but somehow I just felt I had to do it. I was thoroughly enjoying it, too. All of a sudden, I felt someone tapping my shoulder and a cold shiver ran down my spine. I wanted to turn immediately and see who it was, but I just could not move. Even my eyes were feeling heavy. I slowly looked around and was pleasantly surprised to see the entire room filled with at least a hundred oil lamps brilliantly lit.

'Balak, don't you want to meet the Aghoris?' I heard a voice and somehow managed to stand up. When I looked behind, I saw a man smiling at me. 'I am the temple priest and I am here to take you to the Aghori sadhus,' he said.

'What time is it?' I asked, forgetting that I was wearing a watch.

'Balak, it is 11 p.m.! You have been here for the past five hours. I checked on you thrice to see if you were done with your prayers or meditation or whatever it was you were so deeply immersed in,' he said.

'But, sir, you could have . . .' I politely countered.

'Balak, I know I could have, but I was specifically instructed not to disturb you. But then they said they had to see you before their own rituals began. I still want to apologize for disturbing you.' Saying this, he requested me to follow him immediately.

I quickly picked up my bag and started walking behind him. Never in my life had I sat for meditation for those many hours at a stretch. The last time I had been in a seated meditation posture for a lengthy period of time was with my guru on the banks of Mansarovar lake in the Himalayas, and that was for a little more than an hour and a half! In fact, sitting for an hour was more than I could usually take as my legs would get severe cramps. *How was I able to sit in meditation for five whole hours?* I wondered.

'Balak, please be a bit careful, there are snakes and scorpions in and around this part of the forest. This specific area is their feeding ground,' the priest said to me.

'Oh okay! Why this particular place?' I inquired, becoming aware of a certain stench in the air.

'Balak, we are walking through an area where the dead bodies are left to be consumed by wild animals. These bodies are not burnt as is the tradition,' he replied.

'Why is that?' I asked.

'Well, there is a hunter tribe that lives deep inside the forest and they do not believe in burning their dead ones. According to their tradition, the dead person is fed to wild animals and scavenging birds. Interestingly, even reptiles like monitor lizards and snakes as well as scorpions seem to have developed a taste for human corpses. So, this is where the tribal people leave the dead bodies and hence, it is infested almost perpetually with snakes and scorpions. Just follow my path and nothing will happen.'

'But what about the wild animals?'

'Oh, they normally come here only in the wee hours of the morning so we are totally safe from them. What we have to be really careful of is to not step on the snakes and especially the scorpions!'

Fortunately, I had a powerful torch that helped in lighting the path. Finally, after walking through the forested path, we reached a place where I saw some people seated in a circle. As I got closer, I realized these were the Aghori sadhus. I also noticed there was a pyre nearby and it seemed a body was being cremated on it.

'*Shambho Shambho Shambho*!' exclaimed one of the Aghoris. He then stood up and came forward towards me. I could not believe my eyes! He was the same person I had seen in Rishikesh and who I had seen in my dream a year ago.

Before I could say anything, he stretched out his right hand and pinched me at the same place he had pinched me in that dream. '*Yaad aaya* (Do you remember)?'

he exclaimed and burst into loud laughter. He then introduced me to the other sadhus seated there.

'*Achcha*, so this is that same boy?' one of them said.

'*Haan, haan* (Yes),' the Aghori sadhu replied.

Although he had introduced all the others to me, he had not introduced himself.

'What is your name, sir,' I asked him nervously. He burst into hyena-like laughter again and then told me he was the senior-most Aghori in the village and across all the regions close to Haridwar.

'They know me as Maha Sidheshwar Aghori Baba. You may address me as "Sidha babaji", as that is how all my followers and other Aghoris address me.'

I nodded.

'Balak, we are aware that your guru has sent you here to take something for him. But, do you know what that is?' Sidha babaji asked with a half-smile.

I said no and explained that my guru had simply told me to meet the senior Aghori and who would give me something I needed to bring back.

'Yes, that is right. So, let me explain to you what it is you will be taking back to your guru.' Saying this, he took me to the burning pyre. We were just about three feet from it when Sidha babaji walked closer to it, put his left hand directly into the fire and started chanting what sounded like a Sanskrit mantra. This went on for more than a minute and all this time his hand was in the fire. I could literally see it burning! A few minutes later, he pulled his hand out.

To my amazement, he did not have even a single burn mark on his hand and, in fact, it seemed that he was holding something in his palm. He came up to me and asked me to open his palm. As I did that, I was shocked to the core. I saw a flame actually burning on the surface of his palm. He began to chant again, and I saw the flame move up and float in the air. With his right hand, he started making some gestures, and as he did that, the flame shot up high in the sky. I could clearly see it in the darkness. In a flash, the same flame swooped down towards me and struck me directly in the middle of my forehead. My eyes closed automatically and I almost lost my physical balance. I was conscious and, in fact, I was feeling tremendous peace. I really did not know what was happening.

The next thing I remember, I was lying inside a small hut, covered with a woollen blanket. As I opened my eyes, I saw Sidha babaji sitting next to me. Before I could say anything, he gestured to me to keep silent. 'You must be feeling a bit dizzy after what happened. Rest for some more time.'

'Babaji, it is difficult to rest. I am keen to know what exactly happened back there near the burning pyre. The last thing I remember was seeing a flame rise high into the sky from your palm, then swoop towards me and strike me on my forehead. After that, I don't remember anything except for feeling extremely blissful and at peace. In fact, even now as I am speaking to you, I am experiencing the same blissful emotion! I don't feel like resting any more. I want to learn more about you and who you are and by that I mean I want to learn more about the Aghori sadhus.'

'Balak, your main reason for coming here is because you were sent by your guru to fetch something for him. However, you are free to learn as much as you want about us. Let us go to the pyre and I will reveal to you what exactly happened with the flame.' He told me to get up and have a cup of tea and then join him outside the hut near the pyre.

5

Naryogi Baba Pulls Something Out

As we sat near the burning pyre, Sidha babaji began explaining. 'Balak, let me first reveal to you that what you are here for is not to take something physical for your guru. What you will be carrying are three powerful mantras, and the only way for you to be able to deliver them to your guru is if these mantras are embedded into you. And so, what you witnessed and experienced last night, especially when the flame rose high into the sky and then struck you on your forehead, was with the specific purpose of awakening certain energy centres inside your body to enable the mantras to get embedded in you. Having said that, what happened last night was just the first step towards preparing you, and, more importantly, preparing your body to receive the three mantras,' he said.

'Do you mean there will be more steps?' I asked nervously.

'Yes, balak. There will be two more steps, after which you will be ready as well as qualified to receive them. You may think, why not just write these mantras on a piece of paper and have you deliver them to your guru? Well, it is not that easy. First of all, these are three of the seven most powerful mantras on this planet and the only way they can be given to someone is through the process of initiation or embedding into that person's body.'

'But why can't my guru get them directly from you instead of through me?' I asked, and then wondered if I had crossed the line.

'Balak, I think that is a sensible question, so let me answer it. To start with, your guru is unable to personally come to us to get initiated, and we are not allowed to travel to your guru. The only way this can be successfully executed is through a trusted intermediary and in this case, it is you! The process of transferring the three mantras into your guru will be done by you, as he has chosen you for it. Enough of explanations. In another ten minutes, one of the other Aghori babas will take you to a place to activate your spinal cord,' Sidha babaji said.

While all this was being communicated to me, I was simultaneously thinking about my stay in the village and also about calling Rahasya about the new development. Sidha babaji looked at me with a big grin. 'Don't be tense. We have sent him a message that you will be staying here with us.'

As he was saying this, I saw another Aghori baba coming towards us from another direction, probably from the forest. 'Gurudev, everything is ready. I have come to take the boy.'

I got up. This new Aghori baba's name was Naryogi baba. He told me to follow him and we started walking away from the pyre.

Just as I was about to leave, Sidha babaji called me towards him, blessed me and whispered something that took me by surprise. 'Balak, you will see a few things that may shock and scare you to the bone, but I want you to stay as calm as possible, and that will happen by remembering your guru. This will give you the strength to endure the activation process.'

After sharing this with me, Sidha babaji told me to touch his feet, which I assumed was for him to bless me, but when I touched his toes, I felt an electric shock pass through my body. As this was happening, I also felt a hard slap on my back. I was told later that slapping hard was the Aghori way of blessing a person.

I followed Naryogi baba and within ten minutes we were inside a dense jungle. 'Don't get scared! They won't do anything,' he said. I asked him who he was referring to. He did not answer and simply told me to follow him. Interestingly, I was using my torch to navigate through the jungle path, but Naryogi baba had no torch and was practically walking through complete darkness without moonlight as well. *How can he see?* I wondered.

'Balak, I can smell my way through the darkness,' he asserted. I was totally startled—by his seeming to have read my mind and also by his words. I had heard of animals having an acute sense of smell but never a human being. We walked for another fifteen minutes and then he stopped and told me to relax. 'We have reached,' he said. 'Rest for some time and then we will have to get to work.'

At this point in time, the only thought in my mind was to diligently do whatever was going to be asked of me. My mission was to procure something special for my guru and that was all that ran through my mind. Having said that, I must admit that, even as a child, I had always been intrigued by the way the Aghori sadhus lived their life. As I grew older, I began to watch documentaries about them and hence, when my guru asked me if I was keen to visit Kotisurya village and bring something from the Aghori sadhus, I jumped at the opportunity. Added to that, I would never say 'no' to my guru.

By now, I was ready for whatever Naryogi baba had planned for me. I was aware that my spinal cord was going to be a part of some process of activation of the three mantras. 'Are you ready?' Naryogi baba asked. I nodded yes. He then instructed me to take off my shirt and lie on the ground, on my back. He told me that, initially, I could experience a bit of pain, but it would go away in seconds. Also, in an almost threatening tone, Naryogi baba told me not to move an inch as remaining still was extremely important for the activation process to be successful.

'*Shuru karte hai* (Let us start).' Saying this, he lit an oil lamp and placed it close to where my head was and then pulled out something from his jute bag that frightened me completely. I could see him holding something and it was wriggling vigorously. In the light emanating from the lamp, I saw what it was and it made me extremely nervous. Naryogi baba noticed my reaction and told me to relax. 'You must remain calm and not move at all,' he said.

Strangely, I was so numbed with fear that even if I had wanted to move, I wouldn't have been able to. And then he brought that 'thing' close to me and held it over my stomach.

'I am sure you know what this is,' he said with a smile.

Well! I knew and had been bitten by one many years ago while trying to catch it with my fingers. It was a centipede. But this one's size was absolutely baffling to me. The largest or longest ones have been known to grow to lengths of more than twelve inches. But this one was almost two and a half feet long and in terms of its girth, it must have been four inches wide. I watched it being held right over my tummy and its face was just over mine. I was completely motionless and that seemed to impress Naryogi baba.

Just as I was wondering what was going to happen next, to my horror, he actually placed it on me. The moment that happened, I felt it trying to grip my body. I was feeling tickled and scratched at the same time. That's when Naryogi baba said, 'Calm down, friend.'

I initially wondered why he said that as I was already motionless, only to realize that he was not talking to me but to the humungous and extremely creepy looking centipede. Interestingly, as soon as he spoke to the centipede, it stopped wriggling and began to slowly clamp itself to my body. It felt like a strong pinch as the centipede's legs clasped on to my skin. Although it did pain a lot initially, slowly and steadily it subsided and surprisingly, I started feeling extremely soothed. My eyes were open till now, but I could not keep them open any more. It just felt totally relaxing.

Suddenly, I felt something entering through my navel. By the time I could react, something had literally wriggled into my body. Once that happened, Naryogi baba pulled the centipede away from me just before it was going to bite me—at least, to me, that is what it seemed to be planning to do, especially with its almost four-inch fangs just inches away from my neck. It seemed to have become extremely aggressive. I could see its eyes were menacing and furious.

Naryogi baba put the centipede back into his bag and started massaging my stomach. 'It now has to travel from your stomach to your back,' he said to me. I was puzzled and asked him what was inside me.

'I will tell you later,' he replied and continued to massage my stomach. Then, after a few minutes, he told me to turn around and lie on my stomach. Just as I was about to turn, I felt something moving inside me and that is when I realized that something from the centipede had entered my body.

As I lay still, Naryogi baba started shouting some strange words at the top of his voice. It seemed like he was neither speaking nor singing. It was probably a mix of both. After a while, he stopped and asked if I was okay and if I was feeling any pain.

'No,' I replied.

'If and when you feel any pain, do let me know,' he said.

Naryogi baba was sitting beside me, probably waiting for something to happen. Almost half an hour passed and nothing happened except for me lying motionless on my stomach. He stood up, started walking around and seemed a bit perturbed. Just then I heard footsteps. It was like someone walking on dry leaves. I hoped that it was a person and not a wild animal. And then I heard a familiar voice; it was that of Sidha babaji. He was quite angry that the process had not been completed within the stipulated time. They were conversing in Hindi, in a slightly different dialect than the one I was familiar with, but I was able to comprehend most of it.

Sidha babaji came close to me and asked how I was. 'I just spoke to your guru and he was asking about you and how you are doing.'

Knowing that my guru was concerned about me was tremendously inspiring and I felt rejuvenated. Sidha babaji told me that the activation should have happened some time ago but for some reason 'it' had not done its job yet. To me, these words were like Greek, so I stayed silent. I then heard him tell Naryogi baba to apply human ashes specifically over my spinal cord and more specifically on its midpoint, saying that the application of human ashes would complete the activation process soon.

When I heard him say 'human ashes', I felt a chill run through my body. It was just a bit too much for me to have the ashes of a human being applied on me. I knew I could not do much about it, though, and remained calm. Just as Naryogi baba was applying the ashes, I felt a sharp shooting pain exactly at the midpoint of my spinal cord and I groaned in extreme agony. I knew I had to tell him the moment I felt the pain, but it was so acute that I could not say a word. 'It's coming. It's coming out now!' Naryogi baba exclaimed, sounding extremely excited.

I could not bear the agonizing discomfort; it was excruciating. I had no choice but to remain still though. 'Just a few more seconds and you will be fine,' Sidha babaji said to me in an affectionate tone.

As all this was happening to me, the only thing I did was to keep thinking of my guru. I was also chanting the mantra he had initiated me into. Suddenly, I felt something wriggle and this time, it was trying to make its way out from my back. Sidha babaji immediately took lots of human ash in both his palms and began applying it in heaps on the point from where the thing or 'it' had finally come out. As soon as he began applying the ash, all the pain suddenly vanished. It was as though nothing had happened.

'*Har Har Shambho* (hail Lord Shiva),' both Sidha babaji and Naryogi baba exclaimed in high-pitched voices. 'Balak,' Sidha babaji said, 'the second activation is complete. Tomorrow morning, the third and final step in the activation process will be initiated.'

6

A Worm with a Bird's Beak and Lizard's Legs?

After that thing popped out of my spine, I momentarily lost all sensation from the waist down. I thought I had been paralysed. Naryogi baba and Sidha babaji lifted me up and carried me back to the hut. I was not exhausted but quite stunned by all that had just happened to me. I still had one question and I had to get the answer.

'Sidha babaji, what was that "thing" or "it" that you and Naryogi baba were referring to? I think I need to know, especially as, for a good forty minutes, that "it" was inside my body,' I said to him.

Sidha babaji looked at me; rather, he was staring at me as if to ascertain whether I was scared or excited about it. Quite honestly, I was just feeling intrigued. 'Balak, the process that you went through was about opening one particular point in your spine. In our world, we call it the *Gnyaan-Jagataha Bindu* or the 'knowledge–awakening point'. This point had to be opened not metaphorically but literally, and to make that happen, we had to use a special instrument in the form of the kookila worm, as it is the only creature that has the ability to open the Gnyaan-Jagataha Bindu. At least this is the way the Aghori sadhus do it. There are other ways to activate the bindu, but we find this method more effective.'

'But what about the role of the centipede in all this? Why was it kept on my body if it was the worm that did everything?' I asked anxiously. I could not understand why that large and vicious-looking creature was kept on my stomach.

'Balak, you will be surprised to know that the kookila worm lives in the abdomen of this particular species of centipede and nowhere else. The centipede benefits from its presence because the worm eats all the bacteria that may be inside the centipede. The worm also benefits as it gets its food as well as protection from other predators by being inside the centipede's body! To answer your specific question about why this centipede was kept on your stomach, let me say that the only way for the kookila worm to get inside your body was for it to come out of the centipede's body. For this reason, we had to place the centipede on your stomach so the worm could come out and enter your body through the navel. Also, this worm cannot live in the open and can only survive inside the centipede. It was made to enter your body to help open the Gnyaan-Jagataha Bindu from inside and not from out. All this was necessary for us to be able to insert the mantras within you so you can then carry them to your guru,' Sidha babaji explained to me.

'So, where is it now?' I asked.

'Oh, the moment it exited from your body, it died. As I just told you, it cannot live out in the open. We are going to bury it as that is also a part of the tradition. We will be doing that tomorrow morning. If you want to see the kookila worm, I can show it to you.'

'Yes, please. I would love to see it,' I replied excitedly.

Sidha babaji pulled out a small matchbox-sized box and opened its cover. It lay in a curled position and looked like it was completely covered in blood, which obviously was mine. Sidha babaji picked it up and washed it with water for me to get a clearer look at it. The kookila worm looked more like a hairy black caterpillar, but on closer inspection, I realized that this was something very different, especially because this worm had what surely looked like a bird's beak. It was very similar to that of an eagle, but much smaller in size. It also had two legs that looked just like the ones on a lizard!

'What kind of a worm is this, with a bird's beak and lizard's legs?' I asked.

'Balak, this is a very unique creature and is not found anywhere else but in this forest, and that too, only inside the body of this particular species of centipede. What you haven't seen are the extremely small human eyes that this worm has! Get closer to it and you will see them.'

I did as he told me. I went almost an inch away from its face, and that is when I saw its eyes. I was completely taken aback to see that its eyes were exactly like those of a human being.

What on earth is this creature? I asked myself.

'We have to eat and then you have to sleep early because in the morning, you will undergo the final activation,' Sidha babaji said. Naryogi baba walked out and away in another direction, towards another burning pyre.

That night, just before I laid down on the floor to sleep, Sidha babaji applied some gooey paste on the spot from where the worm had crawled out of my spinal cord. He told me that the paste was called *ahooki* and it was made from special forest herbs that would not only prevent infection but heal the wound completely within just a few hours. He also instructed me to sleep either on my stomach or on my side, so as to allow the ahooki paste to work its magic.

Sometime later, I was woken up by Sidha babaji with a bowl of warm water mixed with honey and lemon. 'Balak, drink this. You will like it and it will also give you strength for the next activation process.'

Along with it, he gave me some fruits. He asked me to check my wound and when I touched it, I felt no pain, only a bit of an itch. The puncture wound had completely healed, just as Sidha babaji had told me the previous night.

'It has healed and I don't feel any pain! It's a miracle,' I told him.

He laughed. 'For you it may be a miracle, but for us it is completely normal. Are you ready for the third activation?' he asked with a big smile, and reminded me that I was going through all of this for my guru.

7

'Tadamba', the Mahaghori of the Kaalika Sadhu Sect

It was 3 a.m. and I was ready for my third activation. I had no clue what was going to happen. Sidha babaji had decided not to reveal any specific details to me. He said that doing so would unnecessarily make me nervous. I became all the more anxious when he said that. 'Balak, of the three steps of activation, the third and final one is the most significant as well as a dangerous one. The danger is not the activation process but it has to do with the person who will be executing the process. This person is also an Aghori but not from Kotisurya village. He hails from one of the most ancient caves known as the 'Hoodibhang Goonfa'. These caves are located at the base of one of the Himalayan mountain ranges and are quite close to Rakshasthal, one of the largest lakes in that region. This Aghori is the only one who has developed the spiritual power to execute this particular activation process. He is from an extremely ancient tribe of Aghoris known as the *Kaalika Mahaghori* sadhus. They look a bit different from us but follow very similar rules and traditions. In a way, their tribe is far more advanced than ours. The Kaalika Mahaghori sadhus are also known for their unpredictable temperaments. If they feel disturbed or upset, they have been known to attack and even kill. I have invited this Aghori here specifically to conduct the third process of activation. I am sharing all this with you because you need to be mentally prepared for what you are about to see,' Sidha babaji explained.

When I remained silent, he asked with a naughty smirk, 'Did you get scared?'

'I am a bit scared, but not too much as I have my guru with me,' I told him.

My words made Sidha babaji go silent, and all through the journey, he did not say a single word. In my mind, two things were going on: one was to accomplish the task of carrying the mantra for my guru and the second, to learn and understand more about the life of the Aghoris. I was already getting to know a lot about them through my interactions with Sidha babaji. I did not know where we were going but I was sure that whatever was going to happen would definitely be thrilling.

As I was walking with Sidha babaji, I continuously kept praying to my guru that the process would not be painful.

After walking for almost an hour through the forest, we came across a well. It was quite a big one with a diameter of at least 100 feet. Although we were still inside the forest, the area around the well did not have much vegetation. The time was 4 a.m., but I could see things around in the dim light of the moon. Sidha babaji told me that the well was more than 10,000 years old and was extremely sacred for all the various sects and tribes of the Aghoris. He also told me that this would be the place where the third and final step of the activation would take place. Just as he was telling me this, I heard sounds of water being splashed from inside the well. 'That's Mahaghori Tadamba from the Hoodibhang Goonfa, belonging to the Kaalika Aghori sect. He is the one I was telling you about earlier. He must be meditating inside the well.'

'Inside!' I exclaimed, thinking there was some cave or opening where he sat and meditated.

'Balak, the Mahaghori sadhus meditate under the water. Many of them come here on certain auspicious days and practise extreme forms of meditation inside this well beneath its waters. Tadamba must have also been practising some intense meditation form, especially because he has to conduct the final activation process on you.'

As I listened attentively to Sidha babaji, I saw Sadhu Tadamba walk out, or more accurately, he quite literally jumped out of the well and came charging towards us. He hugged Sidha babaji and began sobbing like a baby. 'Sidha! I'm seeing you after such a long time. You look fit and fine.'

As they were talking to each other, I noticed something peculiar. Tadamba was at least eight feet tall and heavily built. To call him a giant would not be wrong. In fact, his entire body structure was different than ours. He had extremely long arms that stretched down to his knees. He had a big protruding tummy, but what really shook me off balance were his eyes. They were nothing like I had ever seen before. The sclera was not white like it typically is with our eyes. It was dark red, and the pupils were white. It was terrifying. His hair was matted, jet black, and he had woven it into a large bun on top of his head.

I was standing away from both of them and as I looked at Tadamba, I began to slowly walk away backwards.

'*Arré* balak,' Tadamba said, 'why are you getting scared? Don't be afraid. Your guru is my good friend. Both of us stayed in the Himalayan caves and have practised meditation together. Come here.'

The moment he mentioned my guru, I felt less scared. In fact, I felt a sense of happiness and security. I walked up to him and he grabbed me by my wrist. '*Chalo*, let us start.' Saying this, he told Sidha babaji to get 'that thing' and then, holding my hand, he took me in the direction of the well. He climbed over its wall and told me to join him. I looked over and saw a ledge along its inner wall. Tadamba was on it and was waiting for me to join him. 'We will have to sit on this ledge and perform the ritual,' he said.

He told me that before he started the actual process of activation, both of us would have to take a bath. Saying this, he suddenly pushed me over the ledge and into the well. Before I could react, I found myself in the water, which was surprisingly clear till the bottom. Tadamba also jumped in and joined me. 'Come, let us go to the bottom,' he said.

Being a good swimmer, I was quite comfortable and it seemed as though he was aware of this. Both of us dived towards the bottom of the well, which must have been at least thirty feet in depth.

As I was going down, I started to feel a bit of pressure in my chest, but Tadamba had already reached the bottom and was gesturing for me to join him. I somehow reached the bottom and Tadamba immediately blew bubbles out of his mouth. I thought he was playing with me by exhaling and blowing bubbles. By now, I was experiencing a tightness in my chest and feeling an urgent need for oxygen. Just then a large bubble from Tadamba's mouth floated towards me and burst just as it touched my face. Instantly, I lost consciousness. The next thing I remember was me on the ledge lying on my back. Tadamba was sitting on me and by that I mean he was literally seated on my stomach, staring at me with inquisitiveness written all over his face.

'How did I come back up on the ledge?' I somehow managed to ask him. With his entire body weight on me, I was finding it tough to even breathe properly. I wondered why he was sitting on me like that and that's when I saw a needle in his right hand. The sight of the sharp needle got me very afraid. I began wondering if he was going to stab me with it. Instead, he pricked his own finger, his little finger to be precise, and as a drop of blood began to form, he brought his finger over my right eye. With his other hand, he forcefully opened my eye and let the drop of blood fall inside. He did the same to my left eye as well.

Initially, I began to experience a burning sensation in both eyes, but within just a few seconds, it vanished. Tadamba told me to keep my eyes closed. He said that the blood had to get deep inside my eyes. 'Now, open your eyes,' he said, and as I did that, everything looked extremely blurred. Although there was no pain or irritation, I was feeling confused and unsettled, and I started thinking I was going to go blind.

'Don't get nervous. Just wait for some time and you will be able to see clearly,' he said.

I closed my eyes and lay there. Tadamba explained what had happened to me at the bottom of the well. He said that he had purposely created the large air bubble as it had the power to make me lose consciousness. Once that happened, he did a pre-activation ritual. He opened certain cells in my brain by touching my head with the tips of his fingers. He said that for the specific brain cells to get activated, I had to be unconscious and added that this was to enable me to absorb and retain the three mantras I was going to have embedded within me and carry them to my guru. Once that was done, he carried me out of the water and brought me to the ledge. Tadamba went on to explain that the drops of his blood put into my eyes was to prepare them for the activation process.

'So, what next?' I asked him while he still sat on top of me. He was behaving like a child in a very playful mood, but suddenly he stood up and called out to Sidha babaji, who had just returned from somewhere.

'Have you brought it?' Tadamba asked him.

'Yes,' he replied. I was still lying on the ledge and my eyes were still closed but I was listening to their conversation.

'After a while, we need to burn the dead body and for that, preparations need to be made. In the meantime, I will bring him out of the well and begin the third and final step of the activation process.' Hearing them speak about a dead body startled me. Just then, Tadamba told me to come out of the well.

'Can I open my eyes?' I asked him.

'Yes,' he replied.

I slowly got up and tried climbing over the wall, but I could not because my vision was still blurred. I told him I could not see yet. He came close to me and told me to grab his arms. I did that and he swiftly pulled me over the wall of the well. He told me to sit down and relax till he got the fire started. Within the next twenty minutes or so, I began to see the fire burning close to me. I had no clue what was being done. All I wanted was for my vision to clear. Tadamba helped me get closer to the fire. Even through my blurred vision, I was able to see tremendous amounts of smoke emanating from the fire. Sidha babaji was also right there, standing close to me. 'Are your eyes open?' he asked me.

'Yes, but my vision is still blurry and the smoke from the fire is hurting me,' I replied.

'All right, what I want you to do now is open your eyes as wide as you can,' he politely instructed me. I did what he told me to. In a few moments, my eyes started watering incessantly, but to my pleasant surprise, as the smoke got into my eyes, I began to see with extreme clarity. In fact, I was amazed that I could see so clearly, even through the dense smoke. I felt that my eyesight had become even better than before. The burning in my eyes too had completely stopped and so had the watering. 'Balak, the third step of the activation process has been completed. Now, we have to get the three mantras embedded within you.'

Saying this, he told me to stand up and follow him. We walked a few metres towards the entrance of a small cave and as I got closer, I saw a dead body. It had been laid on a burning pyre and was being cremated. 'I am hungry,' Tadamba said. He pulled out a sharp knife and cut out a piece of flesh from the corpse. It was a part of its right thigh. I was aware the Aghoris did this particular thing, but to see it happening in front of me was quite a shock. Quite honestly, until now, I hadn't even seen a body being cremated. I have to admit that the mere sight of Tadamba eating partially burnt human flesh and that too with gusto made me almost throw up.

'Sidha, you too have some of it. The flesh is very tasty.'

Immediately, Sidha babaji took out a *chimpta* (tongs) and pulled out something that looked like the human liver. 'Tadamba, *yeh bahut hi* tasty *hain* (Tadamba, this part is extremely tasty).' Saying this, he gave a part of the seemingly semi-cooked liver to Tadamba and both of them started eating it. I did not know what to do and tried to look away from them. It was just too much for me to see all this happening before me. Yet, somewhere deep down inside me, I felt excited to watch the Aghoris living their life. I had only heard and read about all this, but to see it in front of my eyes was almost unbelievable.

'Balak, *lo tum bhi khao* (Balak, you too have some of it),' Tadamba said to me. I was stunned by his offer and nervously told him no. I was nervous because Sidha babaji had already cautioned me about his unpredictability and his anger as well. I was hoping he would not get upset about my rejecting his offer, but to my surprise, he did not seem to mind. '*Balak, humme pata hain tum yeh sab nahi khate ho. Hum thoda mazak kar rahe thhe* (Balak, I know you don't eat all this stuff. I was just making fun of you).'

I heaved a sigh of relief but at the same time, I was feeling very hungry. I had not eaten anything since the morning tea and fruits I had in the hut. Almost instantly, Tadamba told Sidha babaji to get some fruits for me. Sidha babaji walked away into the forest and I lost sight of him. Then, after a few minutes, he returned with a large watermelon. 'This is a wild watermelon and it is extremely sweet,' Sidha babaji said. He smashed it open with his bare hands, gave me one half of it and threw the other half in the well. 'They too would be hungry,' he said to Tadamba. When I heard these words, I lost a heartbeat. *Who is in that well*, I wondered but before I could think about it, Tadamba reminded me that I had to get ready for the final part, the embedding of the three mantras inside me.

'*Jyada mat socho. Jaldi se tarbooz ko kha lo* (Don't overthink. Finish eating the watermelon fast).' Tadamba seemed to be in a hurry and hence, I gobbled down the watermelon and, as instructed by Sidha babaji, took another dip in the well and returned. By now, the corpse had completely burnt to ashes.

'*Hum tayyar hain* (We are ready to start),' Tadamba said. He told me to hold some ash in my palm and then placed his right palm on it. Along with Sidha babaji, he started chanting something at a high decibel level. '*Yeh raakh ko havve mein oochal do* (Throw the ash high into the air),' he said. I threw all the ash high and something very strange happened. Rather than falling back to the ground, the ash started floating as though it was defying gravity. In the next few seconds, the floating ash had formed what looked like a smoke screen. Tadamba was continuously chanting the same thing aloud and while doing so, he gestured to me to keep staring at the horizontal floating smoke screen.

Initially, it looked like the ash was wedged in space but then something bizarre happened. On that screen of floating ash, I began to see something that looked like syllables in Sanskrit. Having studied the language, although it was many years ago, I was able to recognize it.

'Can you see the symbols?' Sidha babaji asked.

'Yes, very clearly,' I replied.

'Memorize them,' he told me and I started doing that by reading them many times in my mind. Interestingly, as I was reading these syllables, I was simultaneously feeling a strange heat at the place on my forehead where the flame had struck me earlier. A few moments later, I began to experience a strong tingling sensation at the point on my spinal cord from where the kookila worm had exited. Tadamba was continuously chanting something as I was mentally reciting and memorizing the symbols. He then lowered his volume and stopped chanting. Immediately, the smoke screen of ash floating in the air simply collapsed on the forest floor.

'*Ho gaya kaam* (The work is completed), *Har Har Shambho*,' Tadamba exclaimed.

Sidha babaji came and hugged me tight. 'Balak, all the three mantras have been embedded in you. The work is complete and you can go to your guru with them.'

8

Patalnath Baba and Seeking the Blessings of Goddess Kundalini

The entire process was over and the purpose of coming here was accomplished! Sidha babaji also explained to me the way in which I would have to share these three mantras with my guru. He said that I had to simply sit in front of him in complete silence and my guru would extract the mantras through certain techniques that he was proficient in. I literally had to do nothing. Tadamba also told me that the original plan was for my guru to personally come here to Kotisurya to this particular place and receive the mantras, but it became impossible as he was unable to leave the temple and the ashram. The plan had therefore been modified and my guru made the decision to send me to carry the mantras for him.

My purpose in coming to Kotisurya and meeting the Aghori sadhus was achieved and yet I felt dissatisfied—and there was a reason for that. I was still keen to learn and understand more about them and their life. All this time, the primary focus had been on ensuring the successful completion and embedding of the three mantras into me, but now the worm of curiosity within me was wriggling violently. I always had the burning desire to know more about the Aghoris and their ways. I would yearn for personal meetings with my guru and in those meetings, I would ask him questions about them. Swamiji—that was how I addressed my guru—would always call me a curious cat, with a big smile. This is why he must have chosen me to meet the Aghori sadhus and get the three mantras for him. Swamiji never told me what exactly I was supposed to get for him and there must have been some reason for it. I, too, never asked and there may have been some reason for that as well! I guess Swamiji thought that the best way I would learn about the Aghori sadhus would be through interacting with them directly.

By now, all of us were back at the hut, and while Sidha babaji along with Tadamba sat outside near a burning pyre with the other Aghoris, I was inside, listening to their conversation and laughter. Sidha babaji had specifically told me to remain inside the hut and do my meditation. At lunch, I was given some extremely tasty dal and rice, which was cooked over burning wood. I was told later that Naryogi baba used to be a chef in a five-star hotel before he left that life and decided to become an Aghori sadhu.

That night, I wondered what the next course of action was going to be. Quite honestly, I was keen to stay for a longer period of time to know more about the Aghoris, but I had to go back and deliver the package, that is, the three mantras, to my guru.

The next morning, after having tea, I began to get ready to return to Haridwar and then later travel back to my home town to meet my guru. Since the phone network there was not very good, I wasn't able to call my guru to tell him about the success of the mission. Naryogi baba was going to take me to the main market of Kotisurya village and from there, Rahasya would take me to my hotel in Haridwar.

I packed and stepped out of the hut to seek the blessings of all the Aghori sadhus there, and especially of Sidha babaji and Tadamba. As I bent forward and touched Tadamba's feet, I heard him recite a prayer loudly. He then held my shoulders, hugged me and whispered, 'Kaha jaa rahe ho (Where are you going)? There is a lot more that you need to know about us Aghoris. I have already spoken to your guru about this and he has given me permission to take you with me. In a while from now, we will be heading for the Himalayan mountains.'

It was a big surprise for me and Tadamba's words made me tremendously exuberant. I, for sure, hadn't been expecting this! Sidha babaji had told me earlier that Tadamba was unpredictable, but this was a bit too much for me. Was I happy about this new development? Oh yes! I was ecstatic at the opportunity to travel to the Himalayas and that too with a very unique Aghori, or rather a Mahaghori, and to learn more about them. I got the feeling that Tadamba, and even Sidha babaji, had known about my extreme keenness to learn about them. I was already packed and had to wait for only a couple of hours before Tadamba and I left the cremation ground to head for the Himalayan mountains.

At approximately noon, we reached the main village where another Aghori baba was waiting for us. The moment he saw Tadamba, he fell at his feet to seek his blessings. 'Let us leave, Gurudev,' he said, and then we left for Haridwar in a taxi he had already booked for us.

Tadamba, despite being a little more than 8 feet tall, somehow managed to fit into the vehicle.

The plan, as Tadamba told me, was to halt for one night at Haridwar and then proceed to Kedarnath. From there, we were to go to a place known as Bhoogoomba Goonfa (Cave) the place where all the Aghoris and Mahaghoris lived, and where they practised advanced occult tantra meditations and rituals.

'So, are you ready for this new adventure?' Tadamba asked, smiling.

'Absolutely,' I replied excitedly.

As planned, our first halt was in Haridwar. Tadamba and the other Aghori sadhu, who I presumed was his student, got out of the taxi near a cremation ground. They said they were going to spend the night there and told the cab driver to drop me at the hotel. It was 4 p.m. when I reached my hotel. The manager was most thrilled to see me and for good reason. Just before leaving the cremation ground in Kotisurya, I'd had a brief conversation with Sidha babaji and told him about the hotel manager and his predicament. Sidha babaji reacted immediately, saying that these people remembered the Aghoris only when they wanted something. He then picked up some ash from the burning pyre, chanted a few mantras in Sanskrit and put it in my palm. He told me to keep it carefully and give it to the hotel manager.

'He has lot of stress and tension. Give this to him and his levels of concentration and focus will increase and along with that, all his tensions will vanish. The child will surely be born. *Har Har Shambho*,' he said.

I gave the manager the ash, which I had put in a small paper pouch. I also told him what Sidha babaji had told me. The manager was so happy that he invited me to his house for dinner that night and would not take no for an answer.

The next morning, as per Tadamba's instructions, I was outside the cremation ground at 6 a.m. Fortunately, the manager himself dropped me on his motorcycle. It was still dark but I could hear Tadamba's loud voice. He was explaining something to the other Aghori sadhu, whose name I still did not know. He looked young, around eighteen years. He was also very tall, almost 7 feet, but he was lean. He too had very long fingers, just like Tadamba.

By now, both of them were near the cremation ground's entrance. Tadamba told me to join them for a cup of lemon, honey and warm water. The younger Aghori gave me a cup made of clay and told me to drink it in one gulp. 'You will not feel hungry or thirsty for the next twelve hours after drinking this,' he said.

'Thanks . . . I do not know your name,' I said to him, smiling.

'Patalnath baba is my name,' he said.

I finished the drink in one gulp, and we left the cremation ground to head to our next destination, Kedarnath. En route, our first halt was going to be the beautiful and spiritual place of Rishikesh, and then from there we would trek to Kedarnath.

'So, how are we going to Rishikesh?' I asked Patalnath baba.

Tadamba heard my question and intervened. 'Balak, we are going to be taking a shortcut through the jungle. I am sure you are strong enough and will be prepared mentally to walk through treacherous terrain.'

I was expecting something like this and hence, was mentally prepared. Having said that, I was a bit worried about my physical preparedness. Although I used to go for treks during my college days, it had been more than ten years since I had been on one. I think Tadamba may have noticed my slight apprehension and he suddenly blurted out, 'You practise Pranayama, don't you? So, there is no need to be worried. Don't take any tension. You will not have any physical problems!'

He seemed to know what I was thinking and in a way, that did not surprise me much. I had heard from my guru that there are some Aghoris and other meditating monks who have the ability to read other people's thoughts.

Although normally it would take twelve hours to reach Rishikesh, because of the shortcut, which was through forested areas, we reached Rishikesh in only half that time. Tadamba told me that he and Patalnath would be staying in a particular cave close to a temple and asked me if I was okay with joining them there. I was more than excited about sleeping in a cave and immediately said yes.

Tadamba told me that at 3 a.m. the next day he was going to perform a unique puja to seek the blessings of Goddess Kundalini at the temple. He added that he wanted me to assist him and Patalnath during the puja, especially while certain specific rituals were performed.

'Assisting us will also be a way by which you will observe and thereby learn a lot about us Aghoris and especially about how we perform pujas,' he said.

At 10 p.m., we had our dinner just outside the cave. To my pleasant surprise, the dinner was extremely tasty. There was steamed rice with thick lentil curry along with something that looked like meat. I was very sure it was chicken tandoori! Interestingly, Tadamba and Patalnath were having something totally different. On their plates were petals of a flower. As there was no electricity, we had lit a few oil lamps and, due to the absence of proper light, I was not able to see which petals they were. Both Tadamba and Patalnath seemed to be enjoying the taste, as though it was chocolate or some delicious food item.

Then, from his woollen bag, Patalnath pulled out a big bottle of alcohol, opened it and took a few large gulps directly from the bottle. Tadamba too had a few gulps and then said to me, 'I am aware that you drink only beer.' He then stood up, walked inside the cave and after a few moments, came out with two bottles of beer and gave them to me. 'Have the beer quickly, finish your dinner and sleep well as we have to be up by 2 a.m. and start the puja at 3 a.m. sharp.'

The tone and manner in which he said this to me was more of a strict instruction and there was no way I was going to say no to him. As I was figuring out how to open the bottle of beer, Patalnath took it from me and opened it in one go with his teeth. He did the same with the second one later! I was very tired and, to be honest, I quite enjoyed the beers. What was absolutely fascinating was the fact that the beer was extremely cold. To me, this was bizarre. How did Tadamba get beer bottles from inside a cave and that too as cold as those one would get from a refrigerator?

By now, both of them had almost finished their second bottle of alcohol! Suddenly, both of them started dancing around one of the oil lamps and asked me join in. I was quite intoxicated myself and did not hesitate to jump in. The next thing I knew, I was being woken up with cold water being splashed on my face. I looked at my watch and it was 2.30 a.m. I was late. Tadamba and Patalnath had already had their bath. I was not sure if they had slept at all. There was a small stream from where Patalnath had brought water for me for my bath. Interestingly, the container that he used to get the water was made from dry banana leaves, something I was seeing for the first time.

I had to get ready in precisely ten minutes. The puja was supposed to start at 3 a.m. in the temple, which was at least 200 yards from the cave. At approximately 2.40 a.m., I was ready with my bag. Tadamba noticed the bag and told me to keep it in the cave as we would return after performing the puja and then proceed to Kedarnath.

By 2.50 a.m., all of us were at the temple. There was a multitude of oil lamps lit at different places inside and a few were near the entrance. The entire place looked beautiful. Before we entered, Tadamba and Patalnath chanted some mantras and then walked in. I was a bit confused whether to join them or stay outside as I did not know those mantras. Tadamba realized I was still outside and yelled at me to immediately come inside.

It was just the three of us in the temple. Patalnath told me to squat on the floor to the right of the idol of Goddess Kundalini. Immediately after that, they started the puja by lighting some incense sticks and simultaneously, Tadamba began pouring water, at least that was what I thought it was, on the idol. When I looked at it closely, I realized it was bright blue. I was keen to know what it was and just as I was going to ask Patalnath about it, he gave some to me to drink.

'What is it?' I asked anxiously.

'This is the *Trikooti-Triveni Teerth* and it is very sacred. It has the power and purity to cleanse you of all your mental as well as physical impurities. It also tastes amazing, unlike anything you have ever tasted before!' he told me, with a smile on his face.

Patalnath was absolutely right. The blue Trikooti-Triveni Teerth was extremely tasty. It was neither sweet nor bitter and had some kind of fizz to it. I wanted to have more but didn't ask as they had started the puja. I remember Tadamba telling me that I was going to assist them, but I was only made to sit there and watch.

Then, both of them stood up and went outside the temple. After fifteen minutes, I heard them returning and they were almost unrecognizable. They had smeared their entire body with ash. The only place where they did not have ash was their eyes. They had smeared ash even on their long, matted hair. I also noticed that Tadamba had applied red paste all across his large forehead. Their eyes looked all the more striking because of the kajal they had applied beneath them. Were they looking scary? A bit for sure, and intimidating! The gigantic eight-foot Tadamba came inside the temple, prostrated himself in front of the goddess and then began dancing. This dance was not like what I had seen him do the previous night outside the cave. I realized he was doing a *tandav*, an ancient form of dance that was performed first by none other than the great Lord Shiva, especially when He entered a totally different and high state of ecstasy and happiness.

Patalnath and I sat beside each other as Tadamba did the tandav dance. After about fifteen minutes, Patalnath told me to stand up. He gave me two large cups, one contained honey and the other had milk. 'Go close to the goddess and the moment Tadamba starts singing, I want you to start pouring both cups of honey and milk on the goddess. Please remember, you must do this simultaneously and slowly,' he said.

Immediately, I stood up, carefully held the cups, walked towards the idol of the goddess and took my position. It was an extremely unusual sight: this large-framed individual with matted hair, his body completely covered in ash, dancing almost like an Indian classical dancer. His moves were smooth and elegant, even effeminate at times. As he continued to dance, he started singing a bhajan and that is when Patalnath indicated to me to start. I began pouring both the honey and milk together on the head of the goddess. As I was doing this, I was stunned to see the entire idol beginning to glow with a golden hue. The sight was beautiful and majestic. 'She is waking up!' Tadamba said and brought his dance to a halt. He stood there looking at the goddess with deep affection, just like a son would feel for his mother. Tears began to flow and they did not stop. As I observed him, I felt as if he was speaking to her through his eyes. His expressions were changing with different emotions.

Patalnath handed a small woollen bag to Tadamba from which he pulled out flowers and began gently offering them to the goddess. The glow emanating from the idol of the goddess was getting so bright that it illuminated the entire temple. This was an incredible sight—I had never seen something like this before and it was happening right in front of my eyes.

Tadamba then called me to his side and told me to prostrate myself before the goddess and seek whatever I wanted; he whispered that I should not ask for anything materialistic. I folded my hands and prayed to the goddess to bless me with stronger willpower and for more spiritual progress as well as greater association with my guru. I said all this in my mind but Tadamba seemed to have heard me. He looked at me as if to say that he was happy with my demands from the goddess.

Patalnath told me that the puja was complete and it was time to return to the cave. Our stay in Rishikesh was over and we were soon on our way to Kedarnath.

As we were walking towards the main highway, Tadamba asked me if I had some money.

'Yes, I do,' I said, but was a bit confused about why he had suddenly asked for it.

'Do you see that hotel to your right?' I turned to see a hotel with lots of flags, presumably of different countries, on its roof. 'It is mainly for foreign tourists and serves excellent food. I want you to go to the hotel and give the manager three hundred rupees immediately. Come back without saying anything to him. If he asks you the reason, just tell him that I have sent you.'

I quickly went there and, as I entered the reception area, the manager himself came to greet me. He must have thought I was a tourist. Before he could ask me about my room requirements, I pulled out 300 rupees and gave it to him. He looked at me completely baffled.

'What is this for, sir?' he asked me with a confused look.

'Tadamba has sent me here and told me to give you the money,' I said.

Just as I mentioned Tadamba's name, the manager burst out laughing. 'No problem, sir. Now I get it. Tadamba Baba always does this.' He burst out laughing again, leaving me confused.

I almost jogged back and told Tadamba what had happened. Tadamba seemed to empathize with my bewilderment and explained. 'Balak, the money you gave the hotel manager was for the two bottles of beers you had last night.'

'But I don't recall any of us going to this hotel and getting those beers. I also do not remember you sending someone to fetch the bottles! We walked into the cave through the jungle and never entered the town!' I replied in anguish.

Patalnath, who was listening, interjected, 'Balak, if we want something, we don't have to go and get it, we can bring it to us and, of course, we always pay for it later—or rather, you did.'

Shock and confusion were written all over my face. Tadamba said, 'Balak, you will learn everything about this, but slowly.'

9

Dandaka Forest and the Eezhobai Mushrooms

By the time we were out of the main town of Rishikesh, it was 7 a.m. Kedarnath was almost 100 kilometres away and Tadamba was keen to reach not just Kedarnath but the main temple there before sunset, which was expected to happen at 7 p.m. Thus, we had twelve hours to make it to the temple and, thanks to Tadamba, we also had three shortcut options to reach there. Of these, the shortest route was one that involved crossing three rivers, walking through ankle-deep snow for a good four hours as well as trekking over two Himalayan mountains. Was I up for this kind of a hard journey? Well, even if I wasn't, I really had no choice. Having said that, I did feel a sense of strength in my body and especially in my mind, which I believe was infused by the encouraging words of

Tadamba. '*Tu toh aram se kar sakega* (You will be able to complete this journey easily),' he had said to me with great confidence.

There was only one problem though; my footwear. After the first trek from Haridwar to the cave at Rishikesh, the sneakers I was wearing had completely worn out. I could feel my right toe jutting out from the sole. Considering this predicament, embarking on such an arduous journey seemed close to impossible.

It was then that I noticed that both Patalnath and Tadamba were barefoot and had always been that way. *How are they able to walk and that too through treacherous paths without any footwear,* I wondered. As I was thinking about this and also my apprehensions about having to walk with torn shoes for another ten or twelve hours, I heard Tadamba instructing Patalnath to get a tyre from a tyre puncture repair shop. Immediately, he ran towards the town's main market and within the next ten minutes, was back with what looked like an old and almost worn-out tyre.

'We will make soles from this and then sew them to your shoes,' Tadamba said. He pulled out a small, sharp knife and cut out two pieces of the tyre. He then shaped them exactly as per the size of my shoe sole and, pulling out a needle and leather string from the woollen bag, stitched them to the bottom of my shoes. 'Now wear them and tell me how it feels,' he said.

I wore them and, to my surprise, they were perfect. I could not feel any discomfort. In fact, Tadamba said, soles made from tyres were best for trekking especially through rough and wild terrain. Tadamba and Patalnath shouted 'Har Har Shambho' and this time, I too joined in.

We left the beautiful town of Rishikesh and started on our way to Kedarnath. We had to cross a long bridge but instead of doing that, we climbed down to the banks of the river below where a boat was tied to the shore. 'Chalo, let us sit,' Tadamba said. In a few minutes, the three of us were sailing along with the current of the river. Patalnath told me that the river we were on was known as River Deekshika, and that travelling by the river route would lessen the duration to Kedarnath by at least two hours.

As we floated along, I was spellbound by the scenery all around and especially by the multiple peaks of the Himalayan mountain range. I noticed several river dolphins swimming along with us, and at times leaping out of the water and doing somersaults. It was the first time I was seeing river dolphins, and looking at them from up close truly was joyful.

After about forty-five minutes, Tadamba brought the boat to a halt at the riverbank. We had reached a place that was completely surrounded by dense jungle. 'Balak, we have reached the Dandaka forest. This place is known for Tibetan monks, who have lived and meditated in this jungle and have attained spiritual enlightenment. In fact, as we trek through these forests, there is a high likelihood that we may come across some ancient caves and, in them, if you are lucky, we may meet some of the Tibetan monks still living there in deep meditation.'

I was very happy to hear these words from Tadamba.

Patalnath and I tied the boat to a tree and then we started walking in the dense forest. Both Patalnath and Tadamba seemed to know exactly where they were going, and were familiar with the jungle pathways. As instructed by Tadamba, I stayed between the two of them so that I would not lag behind. Tadamba told me that this journey would take a little more than nine hours, but that was much less than the time it would have taken had we gone by the National Highway.

Apart from this, he also cautioned me about possible encounters with wild animals, large fruit-eating bats as well as one of the largest, most rare species of bats known as Seekhoodi bats, which had a reputation for attacking large mammals. Tadamba added that, a few years ago, two people who had come to this forest to make a documentary about these bats were viciously attacked by them. Unfortunately, only one of them managed to survive. The Seekhoodi bats are extremely large, with a wingspan that stretches up to 11 feet, tip to tip. They can glide without flapping their wings even at low altitudes, as low as just a foot above the ground.

Unfortunately, they have a very aggressive mindset and are extremely unpredictable.

'Patalnath and I were also attacked the last time we were here,' Tadamba added. 'But they could not do much as they fear one thing that we possessed and that was the *kali* or black stone, also known as the *Shaligram*. These bats get scared of the Shaligram stone because of certain divine powers it possesses.' He told Patalnath to hand me one. 'Balak, keep this stone in your bag and you'll see that the Seekhoodi bats will not be able to harm you.'

Patalnath took out a Shaligram stone from his bag and gave it first to Tadamba who held it for a few seconds, murmured something—which I assumed was some powerful mantra—and then gave it to me.

The stone looked different. It was an opaque blue but also had a black line across it. Also, the one I held had a lot of rings that seemed to be purposely etched on it. Even its shape was quite peculiar. It looked almost exactly like a red grape though it was around three times larger in size. The texture was extremely smooth and felt soft in my hands; it was very cold as well.

Tadamba told me that although the Shaligram stone was for my protection against the bats, I could keep it with me for the rest of my life. I was exhilarated to hear this, since I always had a deep fascination for collecting ancient artefacts as well as unique stones and rocks. I thanked Tadamba profusely and we continued to trek through the dense forest.

Almost three hours into the trek, we came upon a large, muddy water swamp. Tadamba told me that we had to cross it to reach the other side and also cautioned me about serpents that lived in large numbers in certain parts of the swamp.

'Balak, the serpents of the Dandaka forest and especially the ones who live in this swamp are extremely docile in nature, almost like sea-serpents,' Tadamba said. He told me to watch my every step while crossing the swamp.

'You may feel them move around your feet, and when that happens, just stay calm and don't try to kick them away. Although they are not aggressive, they do have a very potent venom that can kill a human being in less than two minutes. A few people died from their bite when they tried to kick them away.'

Fortunately, we managed to cross the swamp without any hitch, but in my mind, I was keen to see these serpents. As the three of us reached the other side and were about to continue trekking forward, I told Tadamba about my sincere desire to see these serpents. Tadamba looked at me with a naughty smirk. 'What kind of a person are you? You really want to see these serpents? Okay then, we will show them to you,' he said.

We were near the edge of the swamp and I wondered what was going to happen. Patalnath, who had heard my request to see these serpents, walked back into the swamp without wasting time. The waters were knee-deep but extremely muddy and murky, and that made me all the more curious to know how he was going to catch them. Slowly and steadily Patalnath walked towards the middle of the swamp, bent forward and put both his hands inside the swamp. As he did this, he looked towards Tadamba and moved his head as if to suggest something. Immediately, Tadamba pulled out a comb from his bag and started rubbing his fingernails on the tips, from one end to the other. As he began doing this, a weird sound started emanating from the comb. He kept rubbing the comb and making that sound till Patalnath told him to stop with some subtle head motions. 'Got it?' Tadamba asked him.

'I got not one but two,' he replied.

'Chalo balak, come and see the serpents for yourself,' Tadamba said to me.

I stood there eagerly as Patalnath started to walk back slowly towards the edge of the swamp. As he started coming closer, I began to see movement on the surface of the water. Suddenly, a giant serpent hood emerged from the swamp! It looked completely unreal because that serpent's hood was at least six feet wide and its girth must have been at least three feet. The serpent showed itself for a brief period and then dived back into the swamp. After a few minutes, Patalnath walked out of the swamp holding what looked like the tails of the serpents. Tadamba told me to walk back a few yards and not get scared. He reminded me about their non-aggressive nature. Despite Tadamba's assurance about the serpents being passive, I was getting the jitters. I had never seen a serpent with a hood of that size ever in my life.

'These serpents are known as *jal-naga* or water-cobras. They are found here as well as deep inside the Amazon jungles. Patalnath will be letting them loose. If they do come close to you, don't get scared. Stand where you are and remain calm,' Tadamba told me.

To be honest, I was extremely excited up to the point that the serpents were in the swamp, but to have them slither around me was something I was not prepared for. Tadamba must have felt my nervousness and so he quickly walked towards me and wrapped his arm around my shoulders.

'Don't get scared. Remember, balak, if you want to know more about us Aghoris you will have to let go of all your fears. Do you understand?'

Saying this, Tadamba raised his right hand, and with his index finger he tapped me right on the top my head and shouted, '*Har Har Shambho, Aulaakh Niranjan.*' As soon as he did that, I felt all my apprehensions and fears slipping away. I was beginning to feel an extremely high sense of fearlessness.

I noticed the two serpents kept staring at me. Each one of them looked like a large thirty-foot anaconda, but with a head like that of a king cobra. That's exactly how they appeared. Interestingly, their gazing at me was something that made me want to get closer to them. Suddenly, I saw one of them slithering closer to me. I remained calm and stood my ground. The serpent was just about four feet away and in front of me. It started to raise its hood and in a few moments, its hood was at least twenty feet above the ground. I was looking at it and it too was staring straight at me. I was mesmerized by the way its eyes were glued to mine. After a few seconds, the serpent retreated a few metres, then suddenly turned around, slithered away from me and went towards Tadamba.

They too were looking at each other but I was intrigued to see both Tadamba and the serpent swaying in an almost synchronized manner. Surreal would have been an understatement. After the serpents returned to the swamp, Tadamba told me how the Aghoris and especially the Mahaghoris possess a special power to not only understand the thoughts of the jal-nagas but even communicate with them through specific swaying body movements. He said that a few species of cobras, including the jal-nagas, since thousands of years, have been used by spiritual and even alien beings to communicate with some of the earthly sadhus and monks, especially those living in the caves of the Himalayan Mountains.

Now that the serpents were back in the swamp, we decided to move on.

Fortunately, as Patalnath told me, we were ahead of schedule. He said that we could even spend some time exploring rare species of insects and wild flowers in the jungle. He described to me a particular species of wild mushroom which, if eaten raw, could enhance the intensity of meditation to extremely high levels. After he had said this to me, Tadamba told him to collect as many as possible for them and also for the other Mahaghoris back in the cave.

It had been about three hours since we'd moved on from the swamp and I was beginning to feel fatigued, especially since we had crossed two rivers, climbed near a waterfall and also a mountain. Had it not been for the mighty Tadamba and the strength of his arms, I would have slipped and fallen to death at least on three occasions. Both he and Patalnath were excellent rock-climbers and hikers and this despite Tadamba being quite heavily built. Both of them were extremely nimble on their feet and, when it came to using their hands and fingers to grip the wet slippery rocks, they were just like professional mountain climbers. I must say that Tadamba especially was very caring and concerned about my safety and kept checking on me to make sure I was okay.

As we continued to trek through the dense forest, I heard Patalnath shouting to Tadamba, 'Gurudev, in this place, I am one hundred per cent sure we will get the Eezhobai mushrooms.'

The place looked like any other part of the jungle. Just then I saw Patalnath using his bare hands like a shovel to dig through the earth. At specific places, he would dig deep and pull out what looked like bright yellow apple-sized mushrooms. This was the first time I saw mushrooms that grew beneath the ground.

After about fifteen minutes, Patalnath had collected at least a hundred mushrooms.

'Do you have some space in your bag?' Tadamba asked me.

Fortunately, I had a large backpack and lots of empty space. I nodded and immediately both Tadamba and Patalnath put almost half the mushrooms in my bag. It was only when I put the bag back on my shoulders that I realized how heavy it was.

'From now onwards, there will be no climbing. It will be a straight and simple path,' Tadamba said.

I was relieved to hear these words and we resumed our journey towards Kedarnath.

10

The Great Yogi, Sri Shivaghori Adbhootanand Baba

The final part of the trek, as Tadamba had said, was quite relaxing and least stressful to my feet. As it was still daylight, I was enjoying the picturesque surrounding and although we moved out of the densely forested areas, there was still another four hours of hiking to be done along some of the most amazing and captivating snow-clad mountains. Patalnath, with whom I had become very good friends by now, told me that we were quite close to Kedarnath. He added that we had taken this route because we would reach the temple of Kedarnath without having to go through the main town. He explained that it was because of the forest route that our total time to reach the temple was reduced by almost four hours.

As we were walking alongside some of the most beautiful mountain ranges I'd ever seen, I noticed the top of what looked like a temple in the distance.

'Is that the Kedarnath temple?' I asked Patalnath.

'Oh yes,' he exclaimed with excitement and started chanting a prayer spontaneously.

Tadamba, who was walking in front of me also became excited at seeing the temple and joined Patalnath in chanting the prayer. Most likely it was a Shiva prayer. I was not feeling shy any more and joined them but was most surprised with myself, as I was able to chant something that I had never read or heard of in my life!

By the time we reached the temple gates it was almost 8 p.m. Tadamba immediately prostrated himself on the ground. He told me to do the same. We walked inside the temple and although the evening prayers were over, the priest immediately recognized Tadamba and bowed down at his feet.

'*Har Har Mahadev*! I am so happy to see you.' Saying this, the priest pulled him towards the inner sanctum where the divine *Shiva Linga* was.

Patalnath and I stood near the entrance and waited. After a few minutes, the priest came out, apologized for making us wait and respectfully invited us inside the inner sanctum. We were near the main Shiva Linga but Tadamba was nowhere to be seen. I thought there may have been an exit at the back from where he could have gone out. This was the first time I had been to this glorious temple and the feeling I was experiencing was of divinity and peace. I looked around to see where Tadamba was but in vain. Why would he leave us here and go out through the back door, assuming there was a back door?

Just then I heard his voice. '*Har Har Shambho, Har Har Shambho*!!' Exclaiming these words, he came out from somewhere just behind the Shiva Linga. He approached me and told me to prostrate myself before the Shiva Linga and pray for inner peace and spiritual growth. I did what he said and as I stood up, I realized that Patalnath had gone. I was sure he had not left the temple. I had not heard his footsteps moving out of the inner sanctum. He had to be inside the room, but where was he? At that very moment, he emerged from behind the Shiva Linga. It was exactly the same place from where Tadamba had emerged. I was all the more curious about this but was not sure how to ask them. Tadamba was chanting his mantras and was completely immersed in deep meditation. I could not possibly disturb him. Patalnath was in intense conversation with the temple priest. So, I sat in one of the corners of the inner sanctum and started to mentally chant the Mantra Japa. Very quickly I found myself experiencing a colourful vision of what looked like a very old sage or sadhu. He was smiling at me affectionately and then I heard him calling me towards him. I wanted to go but was finding it difficult to do so. That is when I felt someone vigorously shaking my right arm and I was jolted from my meditation. I opened my eyes and saw Tadamba, Patalnath and the priest too, staring at me, intrigued.

'Chalo balak, he is calling you,' Tadamba said.

I got all the more confused and naturally so. Tadamba and Patalnath and the priest were the only people present in that temple and so I wondered who could have been calling me. The priest then came forward, told me to remove my T-shirt and trackpants, and then he began applying heaps of *bhasma*, scented ash, all over my body.

'Don't worry, you are actually very fortunate and blessed to meet him. There is a protocol that we have to follow and it requires a process of covering the entire body with scented ash, for that is the only way he can see you.'

The priest's words left me all the more clueless.

'Sir, you will have to take off your inner wear as well,' the priest said to me and for a few moments, I felt as if the floor beneath me was slipping away. I was extremely reluctant to do as he'd asked. It was then that Tadamba came towards me.

'Balak, the person you are about to meet is a great yogi. His name is Shivaghori Adbhootanand Baba. For the past five thousand years, he has lived beneath this temple and has been practising something known as meditative hibernation. After a hundred years of being in this meditation, he comes out of his hibernation and meets his students. Today is that day, which is exactly why we had to reach the temple today to be able to meet him and seek his blessings. For some special reason, the Baba wants to meet you, but then, you will have to follow the tradition of going there with scented ash all over your body, wearing no clothes including your innerwear. It is a protocol that has been followed for hundreds of years and you will also have to follow it if you want to meet him.'

Tadamba's tone was quite clear, and an opportunity to meet this great soul was too tempting for me to reject. I had always been someone who looked forward to finding and meeting different spiritual people, especially the yogis meditating in the Himalayan mountains, and here was this amazing opportunity to meet a yogi who apparently had been meditating for the past 5000 years. I had heard about such people living inside the Himalayan caves and had also read about Tibetan monks who would sit on high mountain tops and remain there for three years continuously without being in touch with other people. But never had I heard of someone who had been alive for 5000 years.

With these thoughts running through my mind, I got out of my innerwear and with the help of the priest, applied the scented ash all over my body as well as on my face and a lot of it on my hair. I did not know how I looked, but when Patalnath smilingly said to Tadamba that I looked like one of them, I sort of guessed what my appearance was like.

Once I was ready, Tadamba told me to follow him. We walked towards the back of the Shiva Linga and I saw what looked like a fairly large opening through the floor. Tadamba was the first to go through and I followed. There were steps that looked like they were made from wood. As we went further away from the entrance, it started to become dark. At certain points I almost slipped, but the fear of falling on Tadamba made me all the more alert and I held on to the mud walls on the side. The angle was steep but manageable probably because I was barefoot, which helped me get a better grip on the ground.

After a few minutes, I found myself on a plain surface and assumed that we had finally reached the place, but that was not it. We had to walk at least another ten minutes—and then there it was. I would call it a place of brilliant illumination! It truly was spectacular, especially as it was lit with a multitude of lotus-shaped, beautifully carved oil lamps. In fact, the illumination reminded me of the ancient temple inside the cremation ground outside the Kotisurya village. But this was not a temple. It looked like a very old cave.

'Wow!' I spontaneously exclaimed. *Where was the 5000-year-old Adbhootanand Baba*, I wondered. The place looked empty. Before I could ask Tadamba about it, I felt something slither pass me.

'That's my pet and it seems to like you.' This was not Tadamba's voice for sure, I knew, after spending so much time with him. It was someone else. And it could not have been Patalnath either, as his voice was not baritone and husky like the one I was hearing. That's when I realized :it had to be the Baba. I somehow could feel his presence around me and it was extremely intense. Despite the place being brilliantly illuminated, I still could not see what had slithered past my feet. Then came this voice that spoke to me but I couldn't see the speaker at all.

'I am right behind you, Subraiya.'

The moment he said that, I got a bit nervous. Yet, something inside me made me fearlessly turn around and what I saw left me completely awestruck.

Is he even human? I asked myself.

11

Sookshma-Tanaya and the Coloured Ash

I was looking at someone who seemed very different from a typical human being. For starters, the man was taller than even Tadamba. He must have been at least 9 feet tall, and he had a chiselled, muscular body. He was extremely fair and looked like a European or an Anglo-Saxon. What was most interesting about him was his face. He was clean-shaven and there was practically no hair on his body. In fact, he did not even have eyebrows. There was just one large, eye-shaped tika, which seemed to have been made with kumkum, right at the centre of his large forehead. His entire body was covered in blinding white ash, and the fragrance emanating from him felt divine. In fact, the fragrance was far better than the most expensive Gucci or Armani perfumes!

There he was, Adbhootanand Baba, and he was standing just a couple of feet away from me. Despite being six feet, two inches tall, I was gazing up at him as if he was a skyscraper. Tadamba, who was standing next to me, politely nudged me to prostrate myself at the Baba's feet. I immediately did a complete prostration and, as I touched his feet, I felt an electric current strike me. Even as I stood up, I could feel some kind of a current passing all through my body, yet I pretended as though nothing had happened. The current was not painful or discomforting, but was pleasant and intoxicating. By now, I was beginning to feel a bit giddy.

'Sit down, balak,' he said to me in a calming and affectionate tone. As he uttered the words, I noticed something very strange. I realized that the Baba had spoken to me in English, and with perfect fluency.

'After travelling so much on this planet and meeting so many people, it becomes easy to learn a few languages,' he said to me, as if reading my mind.

Tadamba, who was listening to all this, did not look one bit surprised.

Adbhootanand Baba then told Tadamba to get some milk and almonds that were soaked in honey.

'Have it. Don't be shy. You have never been a shy person since the time you met your guru, especially after your trip with him to the Kailash Mansarovar. He had mentioned you at the time we met at the base of Mount Kailash, the same place where he was blessed with the *Atma-Linga*. And so when Tadamba was at Kotisurya, I told him to bring you here so that I could also see your guru's favourite student.'

Saying this, he laughed aloud and added, 'Balak, please remember, for your guru or for any teacher, each and every one of his students is the same. His love is just like the sun's rays that reach every form of existence with the same intensity. It is up to you, as to how much of those rays you want to absorb.'

I listened to his words intently. His voice was extremely calming. Even his gaze towards me was full of motherly love and care. 'By the way, do you know any prayer or even a devotional song?' the Baba asked.

'Yes, I do and I have learnt all of them from my guru,' I replied.

'Then why don't you chant or sing something for Tadamba and me?'

I hesitated for a few seconds but then gathered all my confidence and accepted his request. 'Sure, Babaji,' I responded.

'*Arré wah*, you too have started addressing me as Babaji,' he said, looking at Tadamba.

I smiled and started chanting one of my favourite Shiva prayers known as the Shiv-Tandav *stotra*. There are quite a few verses in that entire chant, and although I hadn't recited it for a long time, I was somehow able to remember each and every verse. As I was chanting the stotra, all of a sudden, the nine-foot sage stood up and started dancing. He seemed to be in joy and ecstasy. I looked to my right and saw Tadamba seated with his eyes closed and hands folded.

The Baba continued to dance till I completed the chanting. He told me to stand up and rubbed his right hand on his head and then, with the same hand, he placed something on my right palm. It felt like a hard stone.

'This is an *Atma-Rudraksh*. It will be a symbol of my affection and connection with you, and it will be with you through a few more of the lives you will be living until you attain *moksha* or complete freedom from life and death towards enlightenment.'

He closed his eyes, chanted something in a very different language, more like powerful syllables, and then, with his left hand, placed something in my left palm.

'This is for your guru. Keep it safe and when you meet him, the first thing you must do without forgetting is present it to him.'

I opened my palm and saw a small glass bottle there. It must have been just about two inches tall and an inch in diameter. Inside it was what looked like a silvery, gooey substance.

'Babaji, may I know what is in this bottle?' I asked humbly.

'It is a semi-solid substance known as *Sookshma-Tanaya*. It is made from the rarest of the Himalayan herbs and is extremely helpful for those monks or spiritual aspirants who desire to meditate for months at a stretch. The Sookshma-Tanaya has certain medicinal properties that will take care of the normal functioning of all the body organs as well as the functioning of the brain cells.

'All that a person has to do is apply just half a drop of it on the forehead, on the eyelids and at the two energy points, namely the navel and the top of the head, which is also known as the *Sahasrara Chakra*. Balak, there will come a time when you will also be using the Sookshma-Tanaya, but for now, I want you to give this to your guru as he needs to practise a form of meditation known as the *Heerambha-Agni Pravartan Dhyan*. This is a type of meditation practice where he has to sit in one place and in one position for three months continuously without even moving an eyelid. Applying the Sookshma-Tanaya will be the only way for that meditation to be successful. So will you be able to take this safely to your guru?' Babaji asked.

'Yes, for sure! I assure you I will take extra care and precautions, and will present it to Swamiji immediately when I meet him,' I replied.

Babaji then looked at Tadamba. 'You please take care of this boy. He will be staying with you in the caves for a few days, right?'

'Yes, Gurudev,' Tadamba answered.

'Show this child who we truly are. Give him a complete picture of our Aghori traditions so that he can share with the entire world what they really need to know. We have, unfortunately, been made infamous for things such as consuming the flesh of dead humans and drinking alcohol. The world needs to know that we, the mighty Aghoris, do far more amazing things that are supreme and spiritual. You and the other senior Aghoris and Mahaghoris at the Bhoogoomba Cave must show him everything about us,' he said assertively to Tadamba.

He turned to me. 'Balak, do you have any questions to ask me? Please don't hesitate. Right now, I am in the mood to answer your questions, so go ahead.' Saying this, he gave me a wide smile. He then closed his eyes and waited.

I looked at Tadamba, wondering what to do.

'Ask whatever you wish to ask,' he said.

I looked towards Babaji and at that very moment, he opened his eyes. His entire facial expression was that of love. He smiled at me as though to pleasantly urge me on to pose my questions. I have to admit there were many questions brewing in my mind and there were some specific ones I felt I had to ask about the Aghori sadhus. But then, after meeting this mysterious and mystical entity Adbhootanand Baba, I felt like asking more about him and his life. I composed my mind and posed my first question.

'Babaji, the first thing I want to know is how you have been alive for such a long time. I mean, five thousand years is beyond my wildest imagination. How are you able to do this?'

Babaji smiled. He then took a deep breath and when I say deep, I mean a *very* deep breath, so much so that I could see his abdomen contract as if it was touching his back. His entire body seemed lifeless and his eyes were so tightly shut, it seemed as if someone had stuck the upper and lower eyelids together with strong glue. The colour of his skin slowly changed from fair to light blue and then his entire body changed to bright yellow.

The only time I had seen a similar thing happening was while watching two creatures, the chameleon and the octopus, change their skin colour. But here was a human being doing something very similar. For almost seven or eight minutes, he remained in that state. On closer observation, I noticed that he was not even breathing. There was absolutely no movement. I looked at Tadamba, but he was in deep meditation; however, in his case, I could see him breathing and the colour of his body hadn't changed at all.

I kept looking at Babaji, and then all of a sudden, he opened his eyes. Suddenly I noticed that his pupils were not even dilating. I then saw him, at an extremely slow pace, exhaling the long breath he had taken earlier. It was very slow and smooth. His eyes focused on me and he smiled.

'Subraiya, what you saw is known as *Sheet-Nidra*. Tadamba may have talked about it to you, but I wanted to give you a literal demonstration of it. To answer your question, therefore, I have been able to live for five thousand years, keeping my body especially fit and healthy, because of this form of meditation. In English, there is a word—hibernation. But this is not the same as the way animals like bears, crocodiles and even insects hibernate. For us, the hibernation is attaining a state of 'external dormancy' while elevating ourselves to higher levels of mental, physiological and spiritual awareness. Just a while ago I gave you the Sookshma-Tanaya, right? Well, there is something known as the *Ateeprabal-Sookshma-Tanaya* and it is at least a thousand times more potent and effective than the Sookshma-Tanaya! I and some other Mahaghoris use this to enable us to remain seated in meditation for at least a hundred years at a stretch. We apply it all over our body, from the top of the head to the tip of the toe. After a hundred years, I come out of this state of Sheet-Nidra or spiritual-hibernation. For a week I am allowed by my Param-Guru or Supreme Spiritual Master to meet my students and other spiritual colleagues as well as to visit other places. This is the time where I even get to exchange experiences with my fellow meditation partners who have also been in hibernation for the same period of time and who come out of it at the same time. This period of one week is also the time when we apply a new coat of the Ateeprabal-Sookshma-Tanaya to prepare us for the next hundred years. I hope I have answered your question.'

'Babaji, thank you so much, but I have a few more to ask,' I said. I was feeling more excited and less apprehensive. Even Tadamba seemed happy, seeing his Gurudev enthusiastically interacting with me.

'Babaji, do you belong to some specific sect or school of yoga? I can see that Tadamba considers you as his guru and so I assume that you must also be an Aghori. But then, if you are one, how are you so different from the others? Unlike all the Aghori babas or sadhus, you do not have the matted hair, you don't wear *rudraksha malas* around your neck and arms. The only common thing I see is the scented ash you apply all over your body just like they do. Add to that your height is beyond unbelievable! Even your face, although it is like ours, is still so different, especially your almond-shaped eyes, the perfect bow-shaped lips. You have ears that look more like those of Mr Spock from my favourite television serial, *Star Trek*.'

I said all this to a person I had met just half an hour ago—someone who was the guru of Tadamba! Had I actually compared him to an alien from a TV show? I was completely filled with embarrassment and Babaji must have sensed that.

'You asked what you felt and there is nothing wrong in that, Subraiya. In fact, this will give me an opportunity to reveal a few things that even Tadamba and some of my other students do not know. Balak, my students are never going to ask me anything except that which has to do with their sadhana or meditation techniques, but thanks to you, at least Tadamba will get to know a few more things about me which he was not aware of until now,' he said, and then went on to explain.

'Let me start by introducing you to my spiritual lineage. I and the other Aghoris like me belong to the *Bhorakshya-Nath Sampradaya* or sect. It is one of the oldest sects in this entire universe. It is older than many spiritual sects across India, the world and even across all the other interstellar realms in this solar system. On this earth, we are called the "Aghoris". The entire Aghori sampradaya is divided into two sects; one is called the Mahaghori sect and the other is called the *Thoombha* sect, about which most people are unaware. Tadamba and some of us belong to the Mahaghori sect. Many of us practise the Sheet-Nidra meditation in some of the deepest and rarest caves in the Himalayan mountains. Some of these caves are so dangerous that even wild animals, insects, birds and bats fear to go in. By the way, Bhoogoomba is one such cave. Tadamba will be taking you there. It is one of the most beautiful caves you will ever see. Once you reach there, you will see many senior Aghori sadhus belonging to both the sects living and meditating there. Having said that, most of us have our own separate caves in which we stay; for example, the one you are seated in is the one that my guru permitted me to be in for a period of seven thousand years. This means that I have another two thousand years to complete my Sheet-Nidra meditation, after which my guru will decide the next course of action for me.

'With regard to your curiosity about the way I look, let me say this. From what I know, there are a few people in this universe who have been born with a pigment that's different from most humans. It is said that entities like us are not completely human. We possess an alien DNA. You may find this quite difficult to believe but only an arrogant person believes that his planet is the only one in this universe that has life on it. To be honest with you, there are so many realms of varied and vibrant existence—only a few are aware of them. Science will take at least another thousand years to realize this and probably another thousand years to develop ways of connecting and interacting with these entities or as you call them, aliens. For now, the power of meditation is the only means to connect with them but that too takes time; in fact, it takes many lives of meditation-practice to be able to learn the techniques to connect with the other realms.

'I believe there is a lot about the Aghoris you will get to see with your own eyes once you stay with them at the Bhoogoomba Cave. At the cremation ground of Kotisurya you saw how the Aghoris consume liquor and eat the flesh of bodies that are literally burning on the pyre. Well, that is just a small and a pleasantly superficial part of the way the Aghoris live their life. But there are a lot of things we Aghoris do to attain what is known as *Shivatva* or becoming one with the Lord of the lords, the great Lord Shiva. Is there anything more you want to know?'

When Babaji asked me this, I paused. He had already told me so much and I was still processing all the information, and I still had a few more questions about the existence of ghosts and spirits and other worlds. But the one question that stood right in front of all the others was if he had ever seen or met the great Lord Shiva. Just as this question was getting formed in my mind, Babaji started responding.

'I have met Him. Mount Kailash is the place He loves the most whenever He comes to Earth and while He is here, He meets the sadhus and monks who have reached advanced levels of meditation or sadhana. Three hundred years ago, when I had awakened from my Sheet-Nidra, He Himself had come here to meet me. In fact, I was seated exactly where you are and Lord Shiva was seated where I am seated right now. He is the ultimate master of meditation and yoga techniques. During that interaction, Lord Shiva taught me a few advanced meditational techniques, especially a technique called the *Vaama-Trataka*. It basically means to continuously stare at the tip of a needle that is kept only half an inch away from the centre of the forehead. It is meant to open the most subtle energy centres that have the power to even make you fly through space.'

Saying this, Babaji told me to come towards him. He looked into my eyes and smiled. He then placed both his palms on my head and exclaimed '*Aulaakh Niranjan*' thrice. As this happened, I could literally feel my mind going completely silent. It wasn't blank for sure. In fact, I started seeing images of a yogi with a blue-coloured body. I knew then that it was Babaji himself.

'Open your eyes,' he said to me while his palms were still on my head. 'So balak, what did you see?' he asked me affectionately.

'You, Babaji. I saw the image of you and your body was blue!' I answered with surety in my voice.

Upon hearing this, he laughed out loud, removed his hands from my head, stood up, bent forward, gave me a tight hug and whispered, 'He was not me. It was Lord Shiva whom you saw in your vision. What you have seen is the real Lord Shiva. I hope that sometime in the future you will get to see and meet Him in real life as well.

'Dear Subraiya, it is time for me to meet some other sadhus. A few are Mahaghoris like me and have come from faraway caves after completing their one hundred years of spiritual-hibernation or Sheet-Nidra. Rest assured, before you return from the Bhoogoomba Cave, I will try my best to come there and meet you. I am sure you will take care of the Sookshma-Tanaya.'

Babaji then instructed Tadamba to take me to the Bhoogoomba Cave and added that he would meet Patalnath a few days later when he visited the cave. I prostrated myself at Babaji's feet and then walked to the wooden ladder. Just then, Tadamba stopped me. 'Balak, that was only to enter this place. Exiting is through another route. Come, follow me.'

We were now on our way to the Bhoogoomba Cave and I was super excited.

12

The Bhoogoomba Cave and the Kushaandi Havan

Tadamba, carrying a small oil lamp, took us through a different exit route which was a long, narrow tunnel. Being extremely tall, he had to bend over quite a bit. It was uncomfortable even for me but fortunately, it took us just ten minutes to exit the cave. I stepped out and saw that we were in a jungle. I looked at my watch and the time was 3 a.m. For some reason, Tadamba extinguished the oil lamp and as he did that, I saw the entire area was lit by the bright moon along with a zillion stars shining brightly over us.

'Come here,' Tadamba said. He was standing a few yards away from me near what seemed like a large rock. He told me climb on it and look towards the tallest Himalayan mountain peak. I was amazed to see snow-capped peaks and among them was one peak that stood taller than the others.

'Yes, I see it,' I said excitedly. Even at that time of the night, I was able to clearly see all the snow-peaked mountains thanks to the multitude of glittering stars across the skies, which added to that beautiful and serene moonlight!

'Balak, our destination, the Bhoogoomba Cave, is situated at the base of the tallest mountain peak you are looking at. It will take us approximately seven hours to reach there,' Tadamba said.

We started our trek through the dense jungle. Fortunately, the path was not treacherous or challenging, at least for the initial three hours, but soon it started becoming tough, especially because the incline began to get steep. We were now trekking at an incline of almost 70 degrees and my legs were beginning to ache, especially my ankles and thighs.

'Let's sit here for a little while,' Tadamba said, smiling at me. He knew I was not at all used to so much trekking, particularly on such steep inclines. I noticed that Tadamba was not tired and even though he was huge, with an extra-large belly, he possessed excellent stamina.

After resting for about twenty minutes and massaging my legs, we resumed our journey. The sun had risen by now and the entire sight was most magnificent. If the night skies had their own resplendence, then the skies in the wee hours of the morning were more breathtaking!

By now we were not too far from the Bhoogoomba Cave and my excitement along with curiosity was skyrocketing. We were trekking through ankle-deep snow and this was slowing my pace considerably. I was baffled to see the ease and speed at which Tadamba was almost galloping through the snow and that too, on bare feet. But then I knew that his kind were different people. They belonged to this place and were born and brought up in this environment, which was completely opposite to where I was from, a concrete jungle. We were also at a very high altitude and this was causing problems in my breathing. That is when I spotted Patalnath standing at a distance. He was waving out to me.

Patalnath had left the temple for the cave much before us through the main temple entrance and therefore must have reached the Bhoogoomba Cave much earlier than us. I was almost out of breath but somehow managed to reach the point where he was standing. He had something in his hand and gave it to me to eat.

'By eating this, all the pain and tiredness will go away and breathing will also become easier for you,' he said.

It looked like the seed of a plum fruit, maroon in colour and interestingly, as I put it in my mouth, it felt like chewing gum. It was minty and sweet to taste. He told me to chew as much as I could so as to squeeze the medicinal juices out of it, but also cautioned me not to swallow. He said it was the chewing gum of the Himalayas and gave me a mischievous smile. Patalnath was right. As soon as I began chewing, its juices began to ooze out in my mouth and I felt my exhaustion swiftly fade away. Even the niggling pain in my knee joints was beginning to dissipate quickly. More importantly, I was able to breathe easily and deeply, and this enabled me to walk at a greater speed.

When he had seen Patalnath, Tadamba had started speeding up towards the cave and in just a few seconds, he had gone inside.

'Can you see something?' Patalnath asked me. I looked to where he was pointing and saw it, a colossal cavity, that was at the base of the mountain—the Bhoogoomba Cave. It was at the base of the same mountain that Tadamba had shown me earlier at 3 a.m. The view of the mountain, especially from such a close range, got me almost off balance.

As we got closer, I realized that describing it as colossal would still be an understatement. I could compare it to entering a large indoor basketball stadium which was two stadiums together, that is how enormous it was. As I entered the cave with Patalnath, the first thing I saw were at least thirty extremely tall men sitting in three rows of ten each, one behind the other. They were seated in a yogic posture known as *Vajrasana* and their upper bodies were bent forward with their foreheads touching the floor. It looked like each one of them was offering his prostration to someone. Patalnath took me further inside the cave towards what looked like a slide heading downwards. 'We have to go down; Tadamba is waiting for us there,' Patalnath said.

He told me that, along with Tadamba, some other Aghoris were eagerly waiting to see me. Apparently, all of these Aghoris knew my guru from the past. Patalnath nudged my back slightly and I found myself sliding down a considerably steep descent, which ended in an almost butt-breaking landing on a wet, muddy floor. Right behind me was Patalnath, but his landing was perfect and I am sure with good reason. For him, this must have been like a daily activity, I assumed.

What I saw in front of me was truly beautiful. It was as though we had landed in an indoor garden with lots of plants and colourful flowers, and in the middle was an ancient-looking structure. It looked like a typical south Indian temple with a large pyramid-shaped roof made out of stone. There were no doors to this structure. Patalnath indicated to me that we had to get inside it. We climbed a few steps in order to get in, and that is when I saw a large pit. In it was a fire burning and around it I saw Tadamba and three other sadhus who looked very similar to him.

Tadamba saw me and indicated with his eyes for me to come and sit near him. Immediately, I gave my bag to Patalnath and joined him. At that moment, the three sadhus looked at me, then raised both their arms and blessed me. Tadamba also did the same and proceeded to explain.

'Balak, for the next seven days, you will be staying with us and will learn lots of things about the Aghoris. What this is, is the fire ritual or *havan* known as *Kushaandi Havan*. This fire ritual is performed every Monday and it strengthens and energizes each and every nerve within our body, which helps us in bettering our meditational practices.'

For the next hour I sat beside Tadamba and witnessed the Kushaandi Havan as it was being performed. What was interesting to see was that, at specific intervals, blue flames would form at the base of the fire, immediately rise as high as twenty feet from the pit and then return to the base. Mysteriously, this would happen only when all the sadhus seated there would chant aloud three words which were, '*Aadesh Jamadagni Aadesh*'. In fact, I was reminded of the time at Kotisurya when a similar looking flame rose high from the Aghori baba's palm and returned to strike my forehead. But in this case, not one but a multitude of blue flames rose together in an almost synchronized manner and dived back to the main fire. It was quite similar to watching a beautiful fountain, especially the one I had seen at a waterpark in Singapore many years ago.

The Kushaandi Havan, as Patalnath later explained to me, was a special fire ritual which was created and started by a great Aghori sadhu named

Aghori Kushaandi more than 50,000 years ago. It is said that Lord Shiva Himself had taught him the ways of performing this particular havan and it is for this reason that the havan had been named after him.

By now my eyes were watering profusely with all the smoke that was emanating from the havan. Tadamba looked at me and realized how uncomfortable I was finding it, and yet he firmly instructed me not to leave. He whispered to me that the smoke was a *prasad* (offering) from the divine spirit of Sage Jamadagni, and it was also filling me with a lot of positive energy and strength. He told me that if I wanted to explore more about the Aghoris and their various spiritual practices, then I had to endure such challenges; facing the smoke was one of the least challenging things.

I was aware that I would witness exciting things in the process of learning about the Aghoris, but to be told that I would have to go through tougher challenges got me a bit tense and nervous. Tadamba must have noticed my expression because he began laughing and said, 'Don't worry! You will not undergo any difficulty or pain; our guru has instructed me to ensure that. In fact, as long as you are with us, you will experience a lot of joy and thrill.'

Saying this, he indicated to me that the Kushaandi Havan was now complete and that I could go and join Patalnath outside the temple.

'How did you find the Kushaandi Havan?' Patalnath asked me eagerly. I told him about the flames and about the discomfort I felt with the dense smoke entering my eyes. He smiled and told me that in the time I'd spend in the Bhoogoomba Cave, I would see many more interesting things about the Aghoris, many of them unknown to the outside world. In the same breath he did tell me there were some practices that were not to be revealed to anyone, especially to outsiders like me.

By now, Patalnath had become a very dear friend and it seemed as though he was assigned the role of taking care of me for the time I was going to be there. He took me to a small cave not too far away from the structure and told me I would be staying there. It was not even a room but just a cavity, about 7 feet by 5 feet. He told me about a beautiful lake 500 yards from the cave, and said I could go there for a swim whenever I wished to.

I was still covered in the scented ash, although a lot of it had come off through the long journey from the Kedarnath temple to the Bhoogoomba Cave. Therefore, what I needed most urgently was a bath. Patalnath said he could bring me hot water but gave me the option of having my bath either with the hot water he would get for me or at a natural hot spring not too far from where we were. In fact, he suggested that I choose the hot spring. But, he cautioned me, before I got all excited, that biting butterflies lived in and around the hot spring.

Upon being told about butterflies that bit people, I did not know whether to be excited or frightened.

'Don't get scared,' he said. 'These butterflies bite only after darkness sets in, so you can go there for your bath any time before sunset. Any time during the day, there is no problem because all of them fly to the mountains and return only after sunset.'

There was enough time for darkness to set in but I decided not to go to the hot spring. Patalnath immediately went and brought me hot water. Before leaving, he wished me well and told me to ask for help any time I needed it. He added that the cavity he was living in was just about 100 feet from where I was going to stay. He told me to be ready by 2.45 in the morning to attend the morning Aghori *aarti* which would start at precisely 3 a.m. He added that Tadamba wanted me to attend it for all the days I would be there.

As Patalnath walked towards his cave, I kept my bag on the floor, unclothed myself and had my hot water bath. It was the most refreshing and relaxing bath I'd had in a very long time.

After that, I lay on the floor and—to be honest—the feeling of laying my back after such a long trek and then being seated continuously for almost two hours during the Kushaandi Havan fire ritual was tremendously relaxing. I do not even remember when my eyes shut and I slipped into deep sleep.

13

Preparing for the Jal-Agni Jagruti

The next morning, at exactly 2 a.m., Patalnath woke me up and told me to get ready for the aarti. He also gave me a few leaves. 'We use them as soap. They will not only cleanse you but also purify your body and mind,' he explained.

'How do I use these leaves?' I asked.

'Oh, that is simple. Just rub them all over your body and as you do that, start pouring water over yourself. That's all! Please hurry, as we don't have a lot of time.' Saying this, he walked away.

I was keen to go to the hot spring to have my bath, but then I realized that there was very little time for that, and because it was still dark, the biting butterflies would be there. The last thing I wanted was to get attacked and bitten by them!

I had my bath and put on the loin cloth that Patalnath had given to me the previous night to wear as part of my attire for the morning aarti. In addition to this, I had been told to apply scented ash all over my body. It was extremely cold and I was shivering badly. I was extremely tempted to pull out the woollen jacket from my bag and wear it even for just a little while. Just then, Patalnath came over and told me to quickly apply the ash.

'Once you put the ash all over your body, all the shivering and shuddering will go away,' he assured me.

Without wasting a second, I put a lot of ash in my palm, added some water, mixed it into a thin paste and began applying it all over my body. I was pleasantly surprised to see that, as I was applying the ash, the cold was steadily going away. Patalnath was there to help me, but he urged me to do the process myself, saying that this would be an activity I would have to do at least twice a day myself.

Finally, I was ready and actually feeling warm despite the temperatures being below freezing, thanks to the scented ash I had applied on my entire body.

I reached the base of the ancient structure along with Patalnath. Tadamba was already inside with forty-five Aghoris and they were all standing in complete silence. One of them looked behind and gestured to Patalnath to come inside and bring me along. As I was climbing the steps to the inner sanctum, I began hearing a humming sound. As I got closer, I saw what was happening. Each of the Aghori sadhus was standing still with hands folded towards what looked like a human skull. Their eyes were open and it looked like they were intently staring at the skull and simultaneously creating the humming sound collectively. The vibration of the humming sound, I must say, was extremely powerful and intense. I noticed that the duration of each 'hum' was almost four minutes, which meant that they were able to hold their breath for that long. I was truly spellbound at the entire sight in front of me.

After about twenty minutes of this, they stopped humming. Tadamba then called me to come and stand next to him. I found myself quite close to the human skull, only a few feet away from it. But I did not feel any fear or nervousness as I had seen grosser things than a mere human skull.

'The aarti will begin now and I want you watch how we perform it,' Tadamba told me.

One of the sadhus standing opposite me raised his right arm towards the skies. I noticed he was holding a human skull and as I looked around, I realized all of them including Tadamba had one. This particular sadhu with his hand held high began shouting 'Aulaakh Niranjan!' and suddenly started to jump up and down vigorously. Each time he jumped high and landed on the floor, he would make the same humming sound, but of a short duration. This happened a few times and then, to my surprise, Tadamba, who was standing beside me, also started doing the same thing. As that happened, all the others started to jump and hum. I was now watching all forty-five Aghoris doing the same action. I noticed even Patalnath was jumping like the other sadhus. They were jumping extremely high in the air and as they landed, they would make that humming sound together. This went on for approximately half an hour and all I could do was watch them with excitement and intrigue. All these 8-feet-tall Aghoris jumping in the air with their right hand raised high holding skulls and that too in a synchronized manner was mystical to my eyes. Something even more unbelievable happened then. For some mysterious reason, I started jumping high into the air as well. After a few jumps, I started not only to enjoy it but also began to feel exuberant. In a few minutes, I was not even aware of what I was doing. My sight was getting hazy and despite this, I still managed to see Tadamba look at me and smile while he was jumping up and down with all of us.

The next thing I knew I was floating on water. My eyes were open and all I could see above were bright blue skies. While I stared at the sky, I started to feel the presence of someone close to me. I was floating but was not sure how. It was as if something or someone was making me float. Although I am a good swimmer, I had never been good at floating on water, especially for long periods of time. *How am I floating like this and where am I?* I wondered. Somehow, I gathered courage and turned to my right. I saw not one but about fifteen other Aghori sadhus floating around me. I was a bit curious and turned to my left, only to see another twelve of them floating on that side.

I was not able to comprehend anything except for the reality of me floating aimlessly. I began to wonder where Patalnath and Tadamba were. These were the only two people I knew and they were not there, at least that is what I thought. Interestingly, it seemed as though I was floating without any problems, like an expert swimmer. The best part was that I was beginning to relax and enjoy the moment. During my childhood, when I used to go swimming, I always tried to float in the water for long periods of time but to no avail, and this, what was happening, was beautifully shocking.

Having said that, I also began to understand that what was happening was also part of some ritual the Aghoris practised. Maybe they wanted me to join them in this ritual. *But where were Tadamba and Patalnath?* I wondered. Just then I heard Tadamba's voice.

'*Har Har Shambho*!' he exclaimed aloud in a tone of excitement. 'Balak, we are performing a preparatory ritual for the main one, known as the Jal-Agni Jagruti or the water-fire awakening ritual. We normally do this once every month on a day and at a time specified by the movements of the sun and the moon. Today is that day and it is wonderful that you are with us to be a part of it. In fact, initially we were thinking of having you witness this ritual, but after seeing your exuberance during the morning aarti and especially the way you became completely engrossed and joined us in the jumping made us decide to have you in this ritual as a participant.'

'But what about this?' I asked, referring to my floating on water.

'Well, this, like I just told you, is all of us getting ourselves mentally and especially physically prepared for the main ritual. During the course of the Jal-Agni Jagruti ritual, we will be required to keep our body floating over the water while certain activities will happen around us as well as on us. I will not tell you more as we have to get ready for the main ritual.'

'Will this take place in this lake itself?' I asked, confident that the answer would be yes.

'Not here but at the hot spring, the same place where you have been keen to have your bath. We have to go there soon and initiate the ritual before it gets dark and the biting butterflies arrive from the high mountains. Although, they too have a role to play in this ritual!' Saying this, he started swimming towards the lake shore and told me to join him soon.

Hearing about this new ritual and that I would be a part of it filled me with a lot of excitement. I was looking forward to it with childlike keenness.

14

Rishi Bruhangnath and the Jal-Agni Jagruti Kriya

By the time I got out of the lake, Tadamba and the rest of the sadhus had already left for the hot spring. Patalnath was waiting to take me there.

I kept wondering about one thing—how had I reached the lake waters directly from the temple? I had absolutely no idea what had happened and how it had happened, and so, while walking along with Patalnath, I asked him about it.

'Balak, this morning while you were jumping with all of us, something happened to you and you started making certain divine gestures and suddenly collapsed to the ground. Just as you were losing consciousness, you were mumbling about how much you love your guru and that you also wanted to learn as much as you could about the Aghori sadhus. Seeing this, Tadamba and some of the other senior sadhus were touched by your perseverance and passion to know about us and so the decision was made to take you to the lake. Not just that, they also decided to make you participate in the Jal-Agni ritual. It is for this reason that you had to go through the floating process.'

I was extremely happy with what Patalnath had said, especially to know that they were pleased with me and my attitude of persistence and sincerity.

By now we had reached the hot spring. It was actually a small, 6 feet by 12 feet pond with lots of hot water bubbling from the bottom. Through its extremely clear and transparent waters, I was able to see the bottom. Tadamba saw me arrive and walked towards me.

'Balak, what I will be sharing with you is extremely secretive and you can only share this with your guru— although he already knows about it. In this main ritual, each of our Aghori sadhus enters the pond, starts floating on his back for a few minutes and then turns to float on his stomach.'

Just as he was about to explain further, I heard one of the Aghoris shouting, 'He has come, make way!'

The moment I heard this, I wondered who it was and began looking around. The place where we were was in a valley, and there was no one I could see for miles around. If he was telling us to make way for someone, where was that person? As I was pondering about this, I noticed a figure. It looked more like a silhouette and it seemed to be radiating white rays. This was mysterious because, just a few seconds ago, I had scanned the same geography but had not seen anything or anyone—and suddenly this silhouette of a human being was walking towards us.

'Who or what is this?' I asked Tadamba, who was standing close to me.

'He is our master. His name is Rishi Bruhangnath. He is also one of those Mahaghoris who has been practising his meditation and penance beneath the divine lake known as the Vishumbhi Tal. He is here to initiate the Jal-Agni Jagruti process, after which he will return to the lake and continue his meditation. He has been living beneath the Vishumbhi Tal for the past three hundred years and will remain there for another seventy years. He will then return to our cave and continue his work of teaching and mentoring all of his disciples, I being one of them. This is all I can tell you for now. Before you ask me what exactly he will be doing as part of the initiation, I feel it is better if you watch it for yourself.'

Saying this, Tadamba walked away from me in the direction of that radiating entity, which was, by now, just about a few hundred yards from where I was standing.

As soon as the rishi came close, Tadamba went on his knees, bent forward and placed both hands on his feet. The rishi then began sprinkling what looked like ash over Tadamba. As he did that, I began to feel slightly intoxicated and dizzy, similar to the way I had felt during the morning aarti. I was about to lose my balance but fortunately, Patalnath held me. He then stood right in front of me, inhaled deeply and, to my shock, he actually exhaled on my face. The moment he did this, all the dizziness vanished.

'You need to be alert, especially now. You are going to be witnessing something spectacular,' Patalnath said.

I nodded to say yes and began watching the entire ritual as it began to unfold.

First, one of the senior-most Aghori sadhus entered the pond, and as he put his first step in the hot spring, all the others began chanting something aloud. Listening to it was really amazing, especially the tune and rhythm in which they were chanting. By now, the senior Aghori sadhu was floating on his back and that was when Rishi Bruhangnath joined the others in the chanting activity. His voice seemed thunderous as it rose above the voices of all the others. This continued for a few minutes and then all of them stopped, and the Aghori sadhu flipped over on to his stomach. His hands were close to his body and he was completely still, like a floating log of wood. Within seconds of this happening, the radiating Rishi Bruhangnath stepped into the hot spring and swam towards the Aghori sadhu. Rishi Bruhangnath completely submerged himself beneath the waters and remained there for at least two and a half minutes. As the water was clear I was able to see him. He was seated in a yogic posture at the bottom of the pond and what happened next took me by complete surprise. The rishi, while in his seated position, raised both his arms straight up and I saw a flame burning on each of his palms. To say it was unreal would be an understatement, and yet that was exactly what was happening in front of my eyes. I was quite literally watching two flames burning on the palms of that great sage as he sat at the bottom of the pond.

I looked around to see if the others were as flabbergasted as I was, but for them, this was an ordinary activity. After a few minutes, Rishi Bruhangnath rose from the bottom of the pond to the surface, came close to the Aghori sadhu's floating body and then he started doing something extremely unusual. With the flames still burning on his palms, he placed his right palm at a particular point on the sadhu's back, on his spinal cord. After that had been done, he did the same but with his left palm. But this time he placed the flame at the bottom of the spine. After doing that, he took a few steps back and slowly retreated towards the pond's edge. The visual of the Aghori sadhu floating on his stomach with flames burning at two points on his spine in a hot spring pond was almost unbelievable for me.

Just then, the floating sadhu started submerging himself underwater and in a few seconds, was almost at the bottom of the pond. I could still see both the

flames that Rishi Bruhangnath had placed on his back
burning fantastically.

How can this actually happen? I whispered to
myself, and decided to seek the answer from either
Tadamba or Patalnath later. After a few minutes, the
sadhu rose to the surface with the flames still burning.
He then flipped over and began floating on his back,
and immediately began chanting some mantra. After
a while, he came out of the pond, went towards Rishi
Bruhangnath and prostrated himself at his feet with
folded hands to seek blessings. I checked to see if the
flames were still burning on his back, but they seemed to
have disappeared. However, I could still tell the points
on his spinal cord where the flames had been placed—
there were bright red spherical marks on those spots.

A couple of hours passed and by now there were just
two Aghori sadhus left to go through the same ritual,
one of whom was Tadamba. As Tadamba was getting
into the pond, Rishi Bruhangnath said something to
him. Tadamba looked towards me and gestured me to
come towards him.

'Balak, Rishi Bruhangnath just told me that he
wishes to give you an opportunity to get into the pond
with me and witness the entire process from up close. I
am sure you have no objection to that.'

I was excited to hear Tadamba's words.

'I will be more than happy,' I responded, my face
expressing the unexplainable thrill I felt. I could not
have asked for more.

Tadamba, after floating for a few moments on his back, flipped over on his stomach and was probably waiting for Rishi Bruhangnath to come and do the needful, and that is exactly what happened. This time, as the rishi sat at the bottom of the pond in deep meditation and then raised both his arms, I saw more than two flames burning on the rishi's palms. In fact, through the clear waters, I spotted four flames on his right palm and three on his left! The rishi slowly rose towards the surface and this time, he began placing all seven flames on seven different points on Tadamba's spine. I observed that all seven points were equidistant from one another. After this process was completed, instead of retreating towards the edge, Rishi Bruhangnath started floating on his stomach along with Tadamba. It looked as if they were floating in a synchronized manner. I was standing near the edge of the pond as that was the only place which was shallow. Just then, something gave me the urge to swim closer to both of them and I did exactly that. In a few seconds, I was just half a foot away from Tadamba. Thanks to the ritual, I was able to stay afloat in the middle of the pond.

I watched them in wonderment. Especially amazing was seeing Tadamba floating on his stomach with the seven flames emanating from his spine. After some time, Tadamba slowly started submerging underwater and, as he reached the bottom, I saw something spectacular. The size of the flames was increasing and they began to rise as high as five feet through the water but in different directions. Tadamba began to rise to the surface, and the seven flames also began fading away.

All this time, Rishi Bruhangnath was still floating on his stomach, but just as Tadamba came to the surface, he flipped on to his back and began floating on one side of his body. Within a few seconds, Tadamba too did the same; he too began floating on his side so both ended up facing each other. This was the first time I had seen someone floating in that way. It seemed impossible but it was really happening!

For a few seconds, both of them stared at each other and it seemed as if they were communicating with each other telepathically. I say this because, while they were exchanging stares, I noticed on a couple of occasions Tadamba nodding as if to say yes.

Tadamba suddenly looked at me. 'Would you like to?' he asked me.

'Would I like to do what?' I asked Tadamba with a confused look on my face. At that very moment, I heard another voice, which was that of Rishi Bruhangnath— and what he said to me sent a cold chill up my spine!

15

Shwas-Roki Keeda or the
Breath-Holding Worm

'Balak, it seems to me that you are truly interested in such rituals and are also enjoying watching them. Right from the time the three mantras were embedded in you by some of my disciples at the Kotisurya cremation ground, I have observed an intense and an ever-increasing desire within you to know more about the Aghori sadhus. What impressed me most about you is the respectful way in which you interacted with the great Mahaghori Adbhootanand when you met him in the cave beneath the Kedarnath temple. Just a few moments ago, while I was at the bottom of the pond, he spoke to me and requested me to have you participate in the Jal-Agni Jagruti process, not as a viewer but as a participant like all the Aghori sadhus. He also suggested that we first ask if you want to go ahead with it or not. Please do not feel pressured to say yes if you are not keen on it. I will accept whatever your decision will be.' Rishi Bruhangnath said this, and then he told me to take a little time to think about it.

Rishi Bruhangnath's proposition was tempting and at the same time, I was a bit nervous especially after seeing what happens in this particular process. I would have flames burning my spine and this thought was giving me the jitters. It was then that Tadamba came towards me.

'Balak, you have come all the way to our cave and I have seen your courage especially when you had to go through some painful processes at Kotisurya. I clearly recall the time when Naryogi baba inserted the worm inside your body through the navel and then when it came out from your spine. Through all this, you were extremely courageous. You endured the pain and that too with a smile. I understand that you went through all that for your guru, but then this too is a golden opportunity for you to actually experience something amazing about the Aghoris. And, by the way, although the Jal-Agni ritual looks quite scary and painful, it actually is not. In fact, after going through this ritual, you would have gained much more than an amazing experience. By sharing all this with you I am not trying to coerce you into saying yes, but I wish to make it clear that this process is not excruciating as you may have assumed it to be.'

As I listened to all this, I got more and more convinced about going for it. I realized that I was getting a once-in-a-lifetime opportunity to become part of their interesting and mysterious rituals. I had to grab this chance and I did so.

'I would love to participate,' I replied to Tadamba and he gave me a reassuring smile.

While all this was happening, I noticed that Rishi Bruhangnath had disappeared and was nowhere to be seen. Well, actually, that was not so because he had already submerged to the bottom of the pond and was seated in a yogic posture.

'Come, let us begin.' Saying this, Tadamba told me to float on my back and in a few seconds, brought his hands beneath my stomach and then suddenly flipped me over. I was now floating on my tummy with my face submerged in the water. Tadamba had told me to take a deep breath and hold it just before he flipped me. For a minute and a half, I was okay but then I began to feel a tightness in my chest. Two minutes had passed by and it was becoming very difficult to continue. Just then, I felt a hand covering my mouth and nose. I knew it had to be Tadamba. He then inserted his fingers in my mouth, opened it and put something in it. Soon enough, I felt something alive and wriggling in my mouth and then, after a few seconds, I felt it going down my throat. As that happened, for some mysterious reason and thankfully so, all the pressure and tightness I was feeling in my chest disappeared.

In fact, I wasn't feeling suffocated at all. I was now able to hold my breath for as much time as I wanted without feeling any kind of discomfort. Slowly and gently, Tadamba held me and took me to the bottom of the pond. I knew the same process that I had seen happening to the other Aghori sadhus was about to happen to me and it made me nervous and excited at the same time. This was all new to me, especially floating at the bottom of a pond, but then, thanks to Tadamba, I was able to maintain my balance.

I felt Rishi Bruhangnath's hand gently massaging my spinal cord and, after a few strokes, I felt some pressure on a point just below the back of my neck. And then, at that very point, I felt a tickling sensation. It was the same feeling you get when someone tickles your feet with the tips of their fingers. I was enjoying it and at the same time, feeling pressure at the base of my spine. A few moments later, I began to experience the same tickling sensation at the base of my spine. I assumed that Rishi Bruhangnath had ignited the fire at these points. Unfortunately, since I was face-down, I was not able to see what he was doing, but I definitely could feel everything, and that feeling was beautiful.

I remained in this floating position for about seven minutes, after which Tadamba brought me back to the surface. I floated for a few more seconds and then Tadamba helped me swim back to the pond's edge. As I walked out, I felt dizzy; however, the tickling sensation at those two points on my spinal cord was only getting

stronger. I told Tadamba about my dizziness and he
assured me that I was not going to lose my balance,
mental or physical.

As I sat near the pond, Patalnath came over and sat
beside me.

'How are you feeling?' he asked me with a bit of
concern on his face. 'No discomfort, right?'

Somehow, although I wanted to reply, I was not
able to. I was trying to speak but it felt as though
something was stuck in my throat. Patalnath noticed
my struggle. He stood up, walked behind me and gave
me a hard whack on my back. Something popped out
of my mouth. That's when I remembered that Tadamba
had put something in my mouth and it had quickly
slipped inside my throat.

There it was, right in front of my eyes. It looked like
a large twig and was probably two and a half inches
long and just about a centimetre wide.

But then, this twig had similar, although smaller,
twigs branching out of the main twig. *What was this
twig doing in my throat,* I wondered. I also remembered
that whatever Tadamba had put in my mouth had
surely wriggled.

I was quite confused and that is when Patalnath,
who was standing next to me, began to make certain
sounds by grinding his teeth. I looked at him wondering
what he was doing. It seemed quite abnormal.

'Don't look at me, Balak, look over there,' he said
and continued grinding his teeth and making unusual

sounds. I immediately turned my gaze towards the twig and to my surprise, it wasn't there! I looked at Patalnath wondering where it had disappeared. With a gesture of his head, Patalnath indicated I should look a bit further. I saw the same twig ahead, crawling away slowly. Patalnath stopped grinding his teeth and began explaining to me.

'Balak, what you see in front of you is not a twig but something that made it possible for you to hold your breath for the entire time you were submerged in the pond.'

'But, what is it?' I asked anxiously.

Just then I saw Rishi Bruhangnath walking towards that thing. He gently picked it up, began grinding his teeth for a few seconds and stopped. He placed it back on the ground. It started moving away and after a few metres, it crawled beneath the snow and disappeared.

'Balak, although it looks like a small twig, it is not. It is a worm that is found only in certain caves as well as beneath the snow. It lives mostly in and around the Himalayan mountainous regions. We call it the *Shwas-Roki Keeda* or the Breath-Holding Worm. There are certain meditational techniques we Aghoris practise that require us to submerge ourselves underwater for periods of time that exceed more than an hour. In fact, there are certain advanced spiritual processes where we have to remain underwater for many years. To make this happen, we need to train and prepare our mind and body for it and this is where we take the help of the Shwas-Roki keeda. This special worm has the ability to slow down our body's metabolism as well as its overall functioning to such levels where, except the brain, the functioning of all the other organs such as the heart, kidneys and liver come to a halt. Remember, we use this keeda only in the initial period to help us train our mind and our physiology, but after a few months of training, we do not use it. In your case, we had to use the worm because a normal person is able to hold their breath for probably two or three minutes at the most. As part of the ritual, you had to be submerged for approximately fifteen minutes, which is why we took the help of this Shwas-Roki keeda.'

I was astounded by what Rishi Bruhangnath had revealed to me. Just then, Tadamba, who was nearby, said something that caught me by surprise.

'Balak, maybe now that you don't have this keeda inside you, I should share something else.' Saying this, he smiled. Patalnath too giggled and Rishi Bruhangnath seemed to have this slightly naughty smirk on his face.

I was baffled and yet was keen to know what Tadamba was going to tell me.

'Balak, the Shwas-Roki keeda may look like a harmless, small twig and may come across as a sluggish worm, yet it is one of the most poisonous creatures on this planet and has a very different way of injecting its venom. The Shwas-Roki keeda doesn't actually bite or sting its prey. All it does is secrete a fluid from its tiny eyes on the body of its prey or enemy. This fluid is the poison that has the potency to kill its victim in a matter of seconds. Unfortunately, it also has a bad temper and even at the slightest disturbance, it becomes aggressive and secretes its poison. A lot of people, while trekking in the Himalayan mountains, have been killed by this creature. Apart from trekkers and mountaineers, two Tibetan monks also succumbed to its poison.'

'How did it kill the humans?' I asked anxiously.

'Balak, this keeda typically lives beneath the snow. It also resides deep inside certain caves. In the case of the Himalayan trekkers, one of them was apparently trying to walk through the snow barefoot and he stepped on it. That's when the keeda got aggressive and secreted the fluid from its eyes on the trekker's foot. I am told that within fifteen seconds, he collapsed and died. However, in the case of the Tibetan monks, it was a totally different situation. These two monks had entered a small cave on the banks of the Himalayan river, Gangotri. Some of the senior Aghori sadhus meditating in nearby caves cautioned them about this particular cave that they had decided to live in. They told the monks that the cave had certain wild mushrooms growing deep inside and they emitted a certain smell that attracted serpents as well as a lot of the Shwas-Roki keedas. They told the monks to find another cave rather than risk their lives. The monks did not pay heed to the words of caution from the Aghori sadhus; they entered the cave and started meditating.

After about a week, a foul smell began to emanate from that very same cave. When a few of the Aghori sadhus went to investigate, they found the dead bodies of the two monks. What was more frightening was to see at least a few hundred of the Shwas-Roki keedas crawling all over their lifeless and decomposing bodies. In fact, it was very difficult to get them out of the cave with the keedas everywhere.'

A big question began to creep up inside me. 'Tadamba, if this is how aggressive and dangerous the Shwas-Roki keeda is, then how come it never attacked me with its poison, especially when it was inside my body? I even saw Rishi Bruhangnath holding it in his fingers and still it did not get aggressive. Why is that?' I asked nervously.

It was not Tadamba but Rishi Bruhangnath who began explaining.

'Balak, it is a good observation and let me answer your question with a question to you. While I was holding it in my hands, did you notice I was doing something peculiar?'

I thought for a few seconds. Initially, I was unable to come up with anything, but then I suddenly remembered that, as he held the keeda, he was grinding his teeth in a peculiar manner. It was happening in a rhythmic way and was extremely unusual. In fact, before him, even Patalnath had done the same.

'Rishi Bruhangnath, I did notice you grinding your teeth and I found that very strange,' I replied.

'You got it right, balak! You will find it interesting to know that this keeda—although aggressive in nature—has a weakness. For some mysterious reason, the sound created by grinding our teeth makes it extremely passive, and it remains this way for at least a couple of hours. The vibration that emanates from that unusual sound seems to pacify the Shwas-Roki keeda and thereby helps us as well. Just before Tadamba put the Shwas-Roki keeda in your mouth, he had made it extremely passive by creating that specific sound. Even now, it is still in a passive state and must be resting deep beneath the snow. It could take another hour or so for it to come out of its trance-like state.'

Learning about such a unique creature as the Shwas-Roki keeda was amazing to say the least, and yet a more fundamental question was forming in my mind. I asked Rishi Bruhangnath,

'Dear Rishi, how exactly did the Shwas-Roki keeda enable me to hold my breath for such a long time? What did it actually do while it was inside my body?'

The rishi smiled and responded, 'Balak, normally these are secrets we do not reveal to outsiders, but you are not really an outsider. You have come here as our guest of honour and so let me answer your question. The Shwas-Roki keeda, apart from having poisonous fluid in its eyes, also possesses a special chemical known in Ayurveda as *Vayukshya*. The sound of grinding not only makes the keeda go into a trance but also makes it release the Vayukshya. This chemical is what generates oxygen on its own and it is this oxygen that made you remain underwater for such a long time. However, the effects of the Vayukshya is limited to an hour. If we want to increase the underwater duration, then all that has to be done is collective grinding. This happens when more than five people grind their teeth together, creating an extremely intense and powerful vibration which makes the Shwas-Roki keeda release the chemical in far greater quantities.'

I was filled with wonder, hearing Rishi Bruhangnath reveal all this to me.

The Jal-Agni Kriya for all the Aghoris as well as for me was completed and I returned to the cave along with Patalnath. When I looked back, I saw Tadamba and Rishi Bruhangnath go the other way, in the direction from where the Rishi had come.

'Tadamba is spending some time with the Rishi, taking instructions on certain advanced meditative practices that he has planned to initiate for himself and a few other Aghoris in the near future,' Patalnath explained. 'Rishi Bruhangnath will then go back beneath the lake to resume his meditation and will return to the hot spring pond only when the next Jal-Agni Kriya takes place.'

That night, I had a bit of pain at the two spots on my spinal cord where the flames had been placed, but it soon dissipated and I fell into a deep slumber and a well-earned rest!

16

Honsagloo Woodpeckers and Shoonya Meditation

The next morning, things were relaxed. I was given permission not to attend the morning aarti as I was extremely tired from the previous night's ritual. I woke up at 10 a.m., and instead of requesting Patalnath to bring me hot water, I went to the hot spring to have my bath. By the time I came back, Patalnath was waiting for me with a half-filled bucket of bhasma.

He said, 'Today is the second day of your stay with us and, compared to yesterday, today's activities will be far more chilled out.' He actually used the words 'chilled out' and I was taken aback.

'*Aaj sab thanda hain* (Everything is chilled today),' he said, laughing.

As he helped me apply the ash over my body, I asked him about the morning aarti. He said that although Tadamba had excused me from attending it, he had come to wake me up. However, since I was in deep sleep, he did not do so. Patalnath seemed a bit concerned about how my stay in the small little cave-cavity was. He asked if I needed anything, like extra blankets or something to munch on at night after dinner.

'Patalnath, the blankets I have are perfect. Even in this extremely cold weather, just one blanket is more than enough. But, with regard to having something to eat at night, I would not mind something to munch on,' I told him.

'Sure. I will bring you some tasty honey-coated roasted almonds and pistachios. Some of the villagers in the valleys below bring them to us once every month. Most of us don't eat them and so we have large amounts stored up.'

'What about you? Why don't you eat it?' I asked, curious.

'Many of us Aghoris living in this cave are being trained by our guru, Rishi Bruhangnath, in certain advanced spiritual tantra practices and therefore we aren't supposed to eat anything that may affect our meditation, not even human flesh.'

Hearing the last two words sent a chill down my spine and my facial expression changed. Patalnath noticed it. 'Come on, don't act all shocked. While at Kotisurya, you have seen it happening, right? Then why are you reacting like that?' he asked.

'Patalnath, it is just that—hearing those words actually made me visualize what I had seen at Kotisurya, and that too at close range. It really was a sight that will remain with me for a very long time,' I explained.

It was around noon and Tadamba, Patalnath and I headed towards the hot spring for a walk. From there, we walked further ahead to the lake where the floating process had taken place. There was snow all around and while walking through it, the one fear I had was of stepping on the Shwas-Roki keeda.

'Don't worry about them, balak. The shoes you are wearing are good enough and will act as protection. Also, remember that they only live beneath the snow that is near the edge of the mountains, not here. So feel free to walk through the snow as there are no keedas here.'

Tadamba's words were reassuring. By now, we had reached the lake shore. There was not a lot of snow there and after picking a spot, the three of us sat down. Patalnath had brought a sheet of plastic, or at least that's what it looked like. On closer examination, I realized it was a large mat that seemed to have been made from thick resin. As I sat on it, I found the surface to be extra warm.

'This mat is made from the latex of the blue gum trees, also known as the *cheekati vruksh*. They grow in the Himalayan forests all year round. Maybe, if we have some free time during your stay, Patalnath will show you the technique by which we use the beaks of

the rare and extremely unique *honsagloo* woodpeckers
to cut into these trees and extract the gum from their
sap. It takes almost three months to make a mat like
this one, but the best part is that it remains in the same
perfect condition for at least fifty years. The one you
are seated on was made by none other than Mahaghori
Bruhangnath and me more than forty years ago,'
Tadamba said. I was most intrigued and wanted to
learn more about the unique honsagloo woodpecker.
I hoped that I would get the opportunity to see that
bird and also see the blue gum tree and the extraction
process.

As I looked at the mountains all around us,
Tadamba requested me to lie on the mat and stare at
the sky.

'For a few minutes, just look at the sky and if
possible, set your gaze towards only one point in the
sky. Try not to look anywhere else. The moment you
are able to do that, a sense of deep tranquillity will fill
every part of your body and mind. You shall experience
something beautiful and serene, which you have never
experienced ever before.'

He too lay on the mat beside me. It was
approximately 12 feet by 14 feet and therefore could
accommodate all three of us easily. I lay down and
began looking at the sky. I fixed my gaze at a specific
point and kept staring at it just as Tadamba had told
me to do. As I continued to gaze, I started to feel a
sense of calmness. The different, vibrant shades of blue

colouring the white skies was a visual that was out of
this world. I felt as though I was floating through the
sky.

Just then, I saw something that looked like a comet
zoom through the sky.

'Did you see that?' I asked Tadamba and Patalnath.

'Yes we did, balak. These are quite common here
in the Himalayas. They come and they go and if you
are lucky or blessed, then you even get to meet them.'

Tadamba's words were mysterious and I was more
curious now.

'Tadamba, your answer has created more questions.
What exactly do you mean by saying they come and go
and that if we are lucky we get to meet them? Who are
the "they" you are referring to? I thought what I saw
was a comet!'

'Balak, for now, all I can say is that you will visit
our cave many more times and I'm sure that many of
your questions will be answered then. Having said
that, I can only reveal to you that our planet is not
the only place in this solar system where life can be
found. Honestly, I cannot say more. You can think
more about this later at the cave.'

I understood partly what Tadamba was trying to
tell me. We spent the next hour by the lake. Patalnath
began explaining to me how he had become an Aghori
and about his life in the Himalayas. He told me about
the times he would come to this very same lake and
meditate through the nights. As he was sharing all this

with me, a question related to the Jal-Agni Kriya began to take shape in my excited mind.

'Tadamba, I noticed something different when you went inside the hot spring to participate in the Jal-Agni Kriya. While Rishi Bruhangnath lit the flames only at two places on the spines of the other Aghori sadhus, when it was your turn, he lit the flames at seven points on your back. Was there some specific reason for this? I'm keen to know.'

Just as I finished, Tadamba looked at me and started laughing aloud. 'You really are an observant and also a persistent kid,' he said to me affectionately. He seemed happy at my keenness and answered. 'Balak, although the main purpose of the Jal-Agni Kriya is to cleanse the mind and, more importantly, the body, this particular process also has another purpose, which is especially for the Aghoris who have accomplished advanced levels of meditation. What really happens when the flames are lit on various places on the spinal cord? Well, fundamentally speaking, these flames are not the same as those you would see burning in a pyre. These are different. They are extremely powerful and even have the ability to not get dowsed by water, which is why, as you would have seen, these flames kept burning vibrantly even under water. These flames are also known as *Adhyatmagni* or spiritual fire. When they are lit on specific points on the spinal cord, all the impurities inside the body literally burn away. Not only that, the flames have the ability and power to burn negative and unwanted thoughts and feelings from the mind. All this leads to a very high level of self-purification.'

'But what about in your case where not two, but seven points on your spine were lit? Why the difference?' I asked.

'You are wonderfully impatient. I will explain. Some of us have been practising highly advanced forms of meditation that require not just purification but awakening of certain energy centres in the body. The object of awakening these centres is to make us go deeper into our yogic meditational practices. The five extra points on my spine were lit for that very reason. I have been practising *Shoonya* meditation for some time now; it requires me to sit in meditation for thirty-six hours in the snow without moving an inch. For this to happen, I have to be able to make my mind very focused and my body very steady. Shoonya actually represents zero, and in a way, it also means total blankness. The lighting of the flames on five extra points on my spine helps me attain the state of Shoonya or complete blankness,' Tadamba explained.

I nodded in understanding, excitement filling my body. I was extremely happy to have gained so much knowledge about the Aghoris and the Mahaghoris.

Later, after spending some more time at the lake shore and listening to Patalnath singing melodious devotional songs, we returned to the cave. On the way back, Tadamba told me that in the evening, after dinner, we would have a *Paramarsh*, a process of interaction where we could ask the senior Aghori sadhus questions and clarify all our doubts. On reaching the cave, he told Patalnath to give me a piece of chalk and a black slate.

'Balak, be ready with your questions. I know you have a lot of them and hence I would like you to write them all on this slate,' he said.

17

The Most Unique Pickle and the Baby Scorpions

Dinner was set up in the upper part of the cave and fifteen Aghori sadhus were going to attend it. It was good to see so many of them seated in a circle eating nonchalantly. Even while eating they kept talking among themselves at extremely high decibel levels. The food was super tasty, especially the combination of steamed rice and potato curry. Along with that, I was offered a thick gooey paste. To be honest, it was probably the tastiest thing I'd had in a long time.

'What is this?' I asked one of the Aghori sadhus seated beside me.

'It is a preparation we call *lonchaeku*. It is very similar to the sweet and sour mango pickle you have at home. But this, although similar in taste, is a bit different and you would have felt it as well,' he replied.

'Oh yes! It is much better in taste than all the pickles I've had,' I said.

'Well, balak, I am glad you liked it; I love it too. Initially, I was not at all keen to even taste it; after all, who would want to eat something that is made from the *kimookuss*. I thought, I can eat anything in this world but not that.'

The Aghori's words got me a bit anxious. 'What is this kimookuss?' I asked. It was surprising to see an Aghori say he was reluctant to eat something, as they are known to eat anything and everything.

'Balak, did Patalnath not tell you about them?' he inquired.

'No,' I answered.

'Oh okay, then let me explain. The kimookuss are the eggs of the bloodsucking botflies.'

I almost spat out the food in my mouth. Some of the other sadhus seated across saw this and began laughing loudly.

'So he knows now why the lonchaeku tastes so good,' said one of the sadhus and all the others started laughing again.

'Balak, you have some left on your plate and you will have to eat it. Every morsel of food is divine for us; we are not allowed to leave anything on the plate. You can leave only after you have eaten everything,' one of the sadhus said.

This was a challenge for me. Eating something made from the eggs of botflies was too much for me.

I sat there looking at the gooey substance wondering what to do. Just then Tadamba walked in and I saw that, except for a couple of senior sadhus, all the others stood up and offered their prostrations to him by shouting aloud, 'Aulaakh Niranjan' thrice.

He walked up to me and looked at my plate.

'Why are you troubling the balak? Why are you not letting him enjoy his dinner?' Tadamba said to the Aghori sadhu who had just explained to me about the lonchaeku. 'Balak, many of these sadhus are very mischievous and will take every opportunity to play pranks on others. The lonchaeku is not made from eggs of botflies as they may have told you. You guys are becoming very predictable. Try using another insect or animal the next time.' Saying this, he also started laughing. 'Listen balak, don't mind them. The lonchaeku is not made from botfly eggs. It is actually prepared using baby scorpions!' Upon hearing this, all the sadhus erupted in infectious laughter.

I did not know what to make of it and looked blankly at Tadamba.

'Balak, I too deserve to pull your leg a bit,' and saying this, he came close to me and told me that the lonchaeku I was having was made very simply by mixing overripe plums, boiled sweet potato, honey extracted from the hives of extremely aggressive wild bees and pure ghee!

'So who and what should I believe, Tadamba? The botfly eggs, the baby scorpions or what you just explained?' I asked nervously, but with a half-smile.

Tadamba smiled, paused for a few seconds, and said, 'Baby scorpions.' As soon as he said that, there was laughter again.

Seeing my perturbed reaction, Tadamba pulled out something from a tiny pouch that was tied to his waist. 'These are the same type of plums that have been used to make the lonchaeku. You must understand one thing. In this cave, we will never feed you anything that will upset you. Also understand that although we follow and practise extreme austerities and meditational techniques and conduct the most challenging rituals, we also love to laugh, have some fun and stay happy. Sometimes, we also play pranks just like the one we played on you. There is a lot you will be learning about the Aghori sadhus tonight and I hope that you have written the questions and doubts that you have on the slate I had given you.'

I nodded, relieved as well as extremely happy about what Tadamba had said.

He told me to finish my dinner and also instructed one of his young disciples to get me more of the lonchaeku, which I happily relished. It was one of the tastiest preparations I had ever had in my entire life. In fact, I was keen to carry some back home, but one of the sadhus told me that its freshness and taste could be preserved only for a day and a half, after which the lonchaeku would start getting stale.

'Can I have the recipe?' I asked eagerly, to which he happily nodded to say yes.

I was sitting in my cave-cavity waiting for Patalnath to take me to their temple to attend the Paramarsh or question-answer session. While waiting there, I started writing about all the experiences I'd had in a small notebook I carried with me. I had just completed the third page when I heard footsteps. It was not Patalnath, but another Aghori sadhu. I had seen him at the upper deck of the cave while having dinner. He was one of those who had laughed the most when I was being pranked and I had noticed him quite clearly at that time.

'Balak, you have been called to the temple. Please bring the slate and chalk along with you. I have been instructed to take you there,' he said to me. This particular sadhu was in charge of the younger ones. As we were walking along, I asked him his age. 'I am nineteen years old,' he answered. I was amazed to hear that. I had estimated him to be about twenty-five.

'Since when have you been living in this cave?' I asked.

'I have been here for the past seven months, but before that I was living in Benares and then for a few years in Kotisurya.' Before I could react, he added, 'Sir, I have met your guru when I was visiting your temple or what you call your *Math* a few years ago. I was there along with my guru,' he told me excitedly.

'Oh really! So you have seen our Math? That is so nice. You said you visited us with your guru. Who is your guru?' I asked him.

'He is Rishi Hatha-Siddhi Nath Baba. He was here with us but had to urgently go to Mount Kailash to meet some senior Aghori sadhus residing near the Mansarovar lake. He left just a few hours before you and Patalnath Baba arrived at the cave. However, I have a feeling that you may still be able to meet him before you leave. I pray that you get the chance to meet an amazingly enlightened soul like my guru. In fact, he too will be extremely glad to see you as he is extremely fond of your guru. There is one more thing you need to know about my guru.'

'What is that?' I asked.

'My guru has recently attained a new siddhi or power. It is known as *Angatrayan* or shape-shifting of his body,' the young Aghori said in a tone of heightened excitement.

This sounded thrilling, but I was unaware of what exactly those words meant.

'My friend, what is the meaning of Angatrayan?' I asked.

'I will tell you. It is the ability of a yogi or sadhu to change his form. What it means is that he can change himself from a human form into anything he wishes to be. He can change from a human into a tree or any animal, bird or even sea creature. This is one of the rarest forms of power which only a few spiritual beings have been able to attain. It requires more than three thousand years of intense meditation practices to attain this particular siddhi,' he said.

'So, are you saying that your guru attained this power after three thousand years? That is insane!' I reacted in shock.

'Sir, what is shocking for you is normal for many of us Aghoris. Please remember, where the subject of science stops is where spirituality starts!' he explained.

For a young man of just nineteen, he was not only mature for his age but also tremendously confident.

As we approached the temple, I saw that Tadamba and some other Aghori sadhus were waiting for me. Just then, the young sadhu whispered in my ear, 'By the way, I wish to apologize to you for the manner in which I was laughing like a mad man while you were having your dinner. I should have controlled myself.' He was very apologetic.

'I did notice you laughing your heart out but I was fine about it. There is really nothing to apologize for. But yes, while I am here, I would be happy to hear more amazing things about the Aghori sadhus—especially about your guru—from you!'

Saying this, I walked up the steps of the temple. The moment Tadamba saw me, he stood up, came close to me and gave me a tight hug.

'You are a very beautiful soul. All the sadhus in this cave have taken a liking to you and are very happy with your genuine attitude of keenness and respectfulness towards all of us. Apart from this, some of my senior colleagues, including my guru, Rishi Bruhangnath have been tremendously impressed with the way in which you have behaved with each and every one of us. Now, come and join us for the question-and-answer session. I can see that the slate you are carrying is completely filled with questions and that to me is a very good thing. Let us start the session!' he said and so started the Paramarsh.

18

Dhoomketu Baba and the Sahasrara Udaan Technique

It was 11 p.m. and the sky had just turned dark. The young Aghori sadhu who had escorted me to the temple was lighting the oil lamps all around us and the entire place was getting beautifully illuminated. I was seated with a group of Aghori sadhus. I could see that, like me, there were a few who had come prepared with questions written on their slates.

I noticed that not all the sadhus were present to participate in the Paramarsh, and was told later that many of them were busy performing their respective spiritual austerities and night meditation techniques.

Sitting next to Tadamba was an Aghori sadhu whom I had not seen before in the cave. He looked very old and therefore I naturally presumed him to be a senior and an advanced sadhu. As we sat in a semicircle, all the Aghori sadhus raised their arms in the air and in one collective voice exclaimed aloud, '*Aulaakh Niranjan*', and like always, they repeated it thrice.

Tadamba began the session by addressing all of us. 'So, as we are here to participate in the Paramarsh session, I wish to introduce to all of you Dhoomketu Baba. The two of us have been contemporaries in the pursuit of spiritual enlightenment. Some of you may have seen him visit me at the cave but for those who are seeing him for the first time, I want to share some interesting aspects about him. Dhoomketu Baba and I started out together as disciples of our revered Gurudev Mahaghori Adbhootanand. We practised basic and advanced spiritual meditation techniques together for more than seventy-five years, after which Gurudev sent Dhoomketu Baba to the Kedar Tal to practise and attain mastery over an ancient and advanced form of meditation known as the Sahasrara Udaan. Mastering this technique of meditation allows you to fly through space, especially towards distant planets across other solar systems and for extremely lengthy periods of time. I have invited him tonight to be with us because today is also the day when both of us met each other for the first time in this very cave. In a way, we are celebrating the special day by being together and also by being with all of you. He will stay with us for a day and then return to Phiran-Mandala after attending day after tomorrow's morning aarti. Dhoomketu Baba is also excited about being at this Paramarsh session. In fact, another reason I requested him to join me here is so that he can answer some of your questions related to our Aghori traditions and ancient meditation techniques. So, let us start. I want our guest to start with his first question. Balak, please state your full name and then pose your question,' Tadamba told me affectionately.

'Yes, Babaji,' I said and continued, 'My name is Subraiya Iyer but I'm fondly called Subbu by my friends and close ones. My first question is, who really are the Aghoris? Most people are under the impression that the Aghori sadhus are aggressive, violent and prefer to live only at cremation grounds. We are told to stay away from them because they drink alcohol and can also get violent. To be honest, until I met Tadamba and some of the other Aghori sadhus or Aghori babas at the cremation ground outside the village of Kotisurya, I really had no idea about your intense spiritual practices. However, through the time I have spent with all of you, I have learnt a lot and it has been truly awe-inspiring! Having said that, there is a question or rather a specific doubt I have and it is about the Aghori sadhus eating human flesh to awaken or enhance supernatural powers within them.'

Tadamba heard me patiently, then closed his eyes and replied, 'Balak, or if I can address you as Subbu, it seemed to me as if you spoke all this in one breath. I sincerely acknowledge your views, observations, your doubts and also your enthusiasm. I will therefore respond to each of your questions, doubts and also your observations in detail. Let me begin. We, the Aghori sadhus, also addressed as Aghori babas, are special types of monks or yogis who follow a different path towards attaining self-realization. Ours is unlike the paths followed by other monks or sadhus belonging to other spiritual traditions. We are followers of Lord Shiva and in Him we also see the presence of the Devi or the goddess. We believe Lord Shiva is the confluence of the masculine and the feminine powers. Are we the only ones who follow Lord Shiva? The answer is a big no, but we are different precisely because of our unusual methods to attain moksha or spiritual enlightenment. "Aghor" is an ancient name of Sanskrit origin. It means a person who is not afraid or fearful of death, who can overcome sense pleasures and undergo the toughest obstacles as well as practise the most arduous techniques of meditation with the singular aim of attaining enlightenment.

'Now, I wish to address the issue related to our food and diet. At the outset, let me tell you that for the Aghori sadhus, food is only a source of sustenance and survival. Consuming the flesh of human corpses— although true—has been overhyped to a great degree. You must understand that we eat other things as well, but what is significant is that we do not make any distinction between the foods that we eat as long as it gives us energy and strength to practise our meditation.

Here, I also wish to throw light on another aspect related to the way we live. The most popular belief is that we only live inside cremation grounds. I don't disagree with that, but the fact of the matter is that we don't live *only* in those places. There are other places too where we spend our lives and these are deep inside jungles, and in caves like the one you are in right now. Then there are some Aghori sadhus who have made their abode beneath lakes. We believe that each place has its own significance and impact on our varied and vibrant meditation practices.

'With respect to cremation grounds, we live there mainly to conquer our innermost fears. Ask any normal person to spend even five minutes in the night at a cremation ground and let me see if they will accept the challenge. But we, the mighty and fearless Aghori sadhus, live there for days and even years. Remember Subbu, our path towards attaining self-realization may appear strange to others but to us it is a sure-shot way to attain self-realization. Having said that, it is also a path that requires complete conquering of fear and anxieties, which is the main reason to live alone in the cremation grounds. Yes! We do encounter disturbed spirits and unknown aggressive entities from other realms while meditating at the cremation grounds, but that itself becomes a test of our courage. There are some sadhus who have even developed special powers to control these spirits, even some of the extremely evil ones, but I have given strict instructions to my disciples not to connect with them. Such powers can actually act as subtle distractions, taking us away from our main pursuit, which is self–realization.

'For us, the frequent consumption of alcohol or incessant smoking of the *chillum* (a hallucinatory drug) along with other things such as pulling partially burnt human corpses directly from burning pyres and eating them almost raw are all the toughest tests of our endurance. Please remember, such things are not part of the usual meditation and spiritual practices we follow. Unfortunately, a lot of people have witnessed only such things and therefore a wrong perception has been created about us being drunkards, cannibals and druggies. For an Aghori, the emotion of fear is something he is trained to burn away as that, in a way, opens the doors to certain types of meditational practices which can take him closer to Lord Shiva and also towards self-realization. For us, our external appearance is totally insignificant and what truly matters is the internal self-discovery and purification. Most people stay away from us assuming that we are aggressive and violent, but then the truth is completely the opposite. Although we surely may appear aggressive and unkempt, we are like other sadhus and monks belonging to other spiritual traditions.

'However, there is one thing about our attitude that is feared justifiably. We have a tendency to feel the emotion of anger but only if and when we are disturbed while doing our meditation. There was one instance when some miscreants began pelting stones at the Aghori sadhus from outside the cremation grounds while they were practising deep tantra meditation. On the first day, these sadhus ignored them but when the same thing happened the next day, they got so angry that, in their uncontrollable anger, they cursed those people to death. Guess what? After three days, partially eaten bodies of two middle-aged men were found near the forest close to the main village. On examination, they found out that wild dogs had attacked these men not far from the cremation grounds. We don't typically use this power to curse but there have been cases like this, where the Aghori sadhu has lost his temper and cursed someone to death. It is also for this reason that you will never find an Aghori mingling with people. He will always live away from them and, in fact, live alone inside the cremation ground.

'Many do not know that we have Aghori temples just like the one you are seated in right now. These temples are spread across India, but you will be astonished to know that many Aghori temples are located in the deep jungles of Peru, Mexico, Brazil; and if this intrigues you, then what I am going to say next will shock you even more. We have seven Aghori temples on seven different planets in our solar system. I am sure you remember, while we were seated at the lake shore, you noticed something zooming through the sky and assumed it to be a comet. Well, it was not a comet but one of our senior Aghori sadhus returning from an

Aghori temple located on another planet. Although we prefer to travel on an astral plane, there are occasions when we need to travel, taking our physical body with us. I am sure these are new revelations to you but rather than telling you to keep all this secret, I would like you to go out there and share it with everybody. More than me, my Gurudev Mahaghori Adbhootanand as well as all the other senior sadhus like Rishi Bruhangnath and even those living on the seven planets are of the strong belief that the right information about us needs to be shared with people in general.

'So, Subbu, I urge you—when you return to civilization, write about us and clear some of the misconceptions that a lot of people have about us. I have shared and hopefully answered most of your questions, if not all, and I hope that you have been satisfied with my explanations.' Saying this, Tadamba raised his arms and proclaimed aloud, '*Aulaakh Niranjan*' thrice.

I said, 'Tadamba, I cannot tell you how happy I am feeling right now. Not only have you made me feel like one of your own but you have also shared so much with me to help me understand and learn more about the amazing Aghor tradition and practices. I promise you that upon my return I shall, after seeking the blessings of my guru, start writing a book about the Aghori sadhus. I know for sure that there is a lot more that I want to learn from you, especially about the Aghori temples on the seven different planets across our solar system, but for now, I am feeling completely fulfilled with the most amazing ocean of knowledge that you have shared, as well as the many things I have experienced myself while living in this wonderful Bhoogoomba Cave. Thank you from the bottom of my heart.'

Hearing this, to my sudden surprise, the senior sadhu seated beside Tadamba, Dhoomketu Baba, came towards me and kissed my forehead. 'You are such a sweet kid. Hey, Tadamba, why don't we induct him into our sect and make him an Aghori sadhu?' he said with a mischievous expression on his face.

Upon hearing this, Tadamba and some of the others started laughing aloud and among them I could hear the one who was laughing the loudest—and we all knew who it was!

19

Brahma-Vatsa-Adrushya Shaligram—The Divine Stone

Did I have more questions? I did have a few; apart from questions on the Aghori temples across the seven planets, I was curious about the various meditational and spiritual practices other than the ones I had witnessed and participated in. But the knowledge I had gained till now about the Aghori sadhus and their life was more than I had ever imagined, and I was happy to let that soak in for now.

In fact, Tadamba's suggestion to write about them in the form of a book had gotten me all the more excited and I couldn't wait to start once I returned home. By the time the Paramarsh session got over, it was 2 a.m.

'Why don't we go for a walk to the lake?' Tadamba suggested, to which all of us enthusiastically agreed.

The entire sky was brilliantly illuminated with millions of stars glittering joyously!

'Subbu, can you tell me what you feel when you look at the sky?' Tadamba asked.

'I haven't seen such a sky ever in my life, never one with so many stars,' I replied in excitement.

'The next time you visit us, I might just take you to one of them,' he said, smiling.

'Really?' I quickly responded. I was not sure whether Tadamba was serious or just pulling my leg.

'If permission is granted by Gurudev, then we can,' he said.

As I sat at the lake shore beneath the almost mind-intoxicating moonlit sky, I started to feel something exceptionally beautiful within me. I was experiencing emotions of heightened ecstasy, something I had never felt before in my life. There was no other thought flowing through my mind other than that of complete happiness and tremendous joy.

As the others slowly started walking back to the cave to rest, I continued to sit there, reluctant to return. Suddenly, I saw the silhouette of someone walking towards me. As it came closer, I noticed something strange about the being. Firstly, I was not even sure if the person was a man or a woman; at least, that is what I felt initially. Despite the moonlight, I found the person's appearance quite blurry and hazy. To be honest, it looked more like an apparition of a human form. When it was approximately ten feet away, it stopped and then I heard a man's voice, which seemed to be speaking to me. I looked around and saw Tadamba and Patalnath almost 100 yards away from me—it couldn't have been them the apparition was speaking to.

'So, you are *Bharadwaj*! In Sanskrit, it is also the name of a bird that lives on your planet. Interestingly, we too have a bird that's quite similar to the Bharadwaj. We call it the *Loombhastal Pakshee*. I can see that you are a spiritual aspirant and that you sincerely practise your *Gayatri Mantra*, chanting in a very disciplined manner. I am truly impressed with this discipline you follow while performing your rituals and divine austerities. You have been initiated into the Mantra Japa by your guru and I am extremely proud of you for chanting this japa every day without fail. I have told your guru that as well,' he said.

I was not sure who this person was, though he seemed to know a lot about me. To add to everything, he did not even have a physical body like ours. He did have the form, or probably a better word could be 'shape', of a human being but he seemed to be made of white smoke.

He continued, '*Sandhya-Vandan* is a very important spiritual practice which people from your tradition and spiritual lineage must practise daily. It quite literally awakens tremendous amounts of positive energy and enhances the power of concentration. I am keen that when you return home, you will spread the importance of Mantra Japa to all the spiritual aspirants you know. I know, at this very moment, you must be wondering who I am. Well, I don't want you to feel confused. My name is Bhambhole Baba. I live in the Maharambha Cave, about fifty kilometres from here. I have come here to bless you, as well as to give you something for your guru. He has been wanting it for many years, and I too have been trying to give it to him for a very long time.'

'What do you wish me to carry to my guru?' I asked curiously.

'Dear, have you heard about the Shaligram?'

'Yes, I have. In fact, during my trip to Kailash Mansarovar along with my guru, I had actually found one on the banks of River Brahmaputra. At that time, I just saw it as a very smooth textured stone that was jet black. It stood out from the others. It was only when my guru noticed me playing with it that he checked it out and told me that it was a special stone. He said that it was a Shaligram and told me to take care of it and not play with it. For some time I kept it with me and then gave it to my guru. And then, at Dandaka forest, Tadamba and Patalnath gave me a blue Shaligram stone for protection from the Seekhoodi bats, which I could keep for life,' I said.

'Balak, there is a lot that you will be made aware of regarding this divine stone called Shaligram later in your life. This particular Shaligram for your guru is one of the rarest of the rare stones and is called the

Brahma-Vatsa-Adrushya Shaligram.' Saying this, he stretched his hand towards me and opened his palm. He held a stone from which a bright golden glow was emanating. The rays coming out of the Shaligram stone were so strong that I was unable to see the stone itself.

'Oh wow!' I exclaimed.

Bhambhole Baba then moved closer to me. 'Here, take this and when you meet your guru, give it to him. I have told Tadamba to give you a small box to help you carry it safe and sound. I have something for you as well.' He opened his other palm. 'This is the feather of the Loombhastal Pakshee. It will always remind you of your meeting with me and the special interaction that is happening between us at this very moment.'

'Did you say that this bird belongs to another planet?' I asked anxiously.

'Yes it does,' he answered.

'Then, how do you have this feather?'

'Well, balak, that's because I too am not from here. I belong to the same planet on which the Loombhastal Pakshee lives! Dear, there are some things you will take time to understand. I must go now, but the next time you come to visit the Aghoris at the Bhoogoomba Cave, I will request Tadamba to bring you to my cave. Maybe from my cave we could travel to my planet and also see the Loombhastal Pakshee.'

Bhambhole Baba started moving away from me but I noticed that he wasn't even walking. It was as though he was a foot above the ground and was floating

away smoothly. I heard him exclaim aloud the words
'*Aulaakh Niranjan*' and then he vanished into thin air.

'Come here, balak.' It was Tadamba. 'Before we
return to the cave, I need you to please remember a
few things. When you return home, the first thing you
have to do is go and meet your guru and immediately
give him this Shaligram. Also, remember that you have
the sacred mantras embedded in you which your guru
is aware of and will extract from you through his own
ways. And finally, as you go back to living your life,
see to it that you share all the various aspects about
the Aghoris. I want you to fearlessly and passionately
start documenting all your experiences and knowledge
about us and then let the world know who we truly are.

'The encounter you had just now will be one of
the most amazing moments of your life. Probably,
it is the first time that you have actually seen, met
and interacted with an alien entity, and that too, a
spiritually enlightened one. Cherish the memory of
this special encounter with the entity for as long as
you can. I believe this entity plans to take you to his
planet, and if that happens, I think it will be the first
time that a human being, who isn't an Aghori, would
have actually travelled though interstellar space to
another planet.

'Dear Subbu, in a few days from now, you will be
back to your pleasantly ordinary life, but if and when
you wish to visit us, feel free to come and stay with
us in our Bhoogoomba Cave. All the Aghori sadhus

living here have taken a liking to you, and some even want you to become an Aghori sadhu. You still have a few days with us before you go back, and so I feel that from now onwards, I want you to spend a lot of time with the mountains. By that I mean what I want you to do is be among them and meditate as much as you can while you are amidst them. In fact, you could practise intensely the chanting of your Mantra Japa which your guru has initiated you into.

'Balak, the amount of knowledge you have absorbed about the Aghoris is more than you yourself could have imagined and I feel it is time for you to focus on your own spiritual advancement.'

Tadamba's words were extremely motivating. 'I give you my word. From tomorrow onwards till my final day at the Bhoogoomba Cave, I will do my Mantra Japa and also chant the Gayatri Mantra more intensely, with a higher number of repetitions,' I said.

Tadamba smiled and patted me on my back affectionately.

By the time we returned to the cave, the sun had risen. I still managed to catch a short nap and then was up for breakfast. The next three days passed smoothly and finally the day arrived when I had to leave the Bhoogoomba Cave. Patalnath and Tadamba accompanied me on my return journey. Finally, at the Kedarnath temple, I said my farewell to both of them and headed directly to Delhi. I stayed at a friend's house for a day and then headed to Pune, my home.

There was tremendous excitement within me about meeting my guru, Swamiji. I sent him a message about my keenness to meet him at the earliest as I was very eager to deliver the three mantras along with the precious things Bhambhole Baba and Rishi Adbhootanand had sent for him, and also to share all my experiences!

Within a couple of days of my return to Pune, I was already on my way to my native village to meet my guru. As I entered the meeting room of the temple, I saw Swamiji seated with his eyes closed.

'Subbu! Or should I also start addressing you as Balak?' he said to me with a mischievous smile.

I immediately prostrated myself at Swamiji's feet to seek his blessings.

'Before you start telling me about all your exciting adventures and experiences, I wish to let you know that tomorrow at 4 a.m., there will be a small ritual involving the extraction of the three mantras from your body. This will be done through certain techniques that I will be performing myself. The correct word for this process of extraction is "transference",' he said.

After that, he started inquiring about the Shaligram and asked me about the Sookshma-Tanaya which Rishi Adbhootanand had sent for him.

That night, Swamiji took me along with a few other devotees to a forested area a few kilometres away from the temple. There, we sat down together and Swamiji excitedly requested me to share each and every adventure and ritual that I had either witnessed or participated in with the Aghoris.

Just as I was about to start sharing everything, from a distance I heard the words '*Aulaakh Niranjan*' being uttered aloud thrice! The words had me completely frozen in shock! Who was it?

Scan QR code to access the
Penguin Random House India website